# Xen

Ancient English Edition
Complete and Unexpurgated
Translated by
D.J. Solomon

Avar Press

ISBN: 0-9760660-0-9



10 9 8 7 6 5 4 3 2



Avar Press.

To LKS,
Who else?

# Contents

## Acknowledgements

THE TRANSLATOR WISHES to direct the reader to two invaluable sources that aided this endeavor: John Keegan's, A History of Warfare, New York, Alfred A. Knopf, 1993, 432 pages and George Ryley Scott's, A History of Torture, first published London, T. Werner Laurie, 1940, reprinted London, Senate Studio Editions Ltd, 1995, 328 pages. With regard to the latter, it is bewildering to think that the very methods that the author was cataloguing, remote and antiquated in their presentation, were in those very years of manuscript preparation and the first years of publication in active use by various megalomaniacs; and his very premise was the evolution of society so as to arise above the need for torture!

The translator further wishes to extend love and thanks to J.H. Solomon for her meticulous editing and is especially delighted that she continues to speak to him after completion of her job. The perusal and informative discussions of the manuscript by L.K. Solomon, I.H.S. Solomon & B.C. Solomon were also most helpful.

# Translator's Note:

THIS IS OF course not THE Ancient English translation, since it will serve as one of several now available to the reader and student of this mercurial tongue. So immediately you may assume that you have been bilked into wasting your time on a version not having passed the test of generations of scholars' analysis; let alone be compared to the Original edition, in our ecumenical Eartherian, which serves as the sine qua non. Publication of the Original version of Xen was quickly followed by translations into all previous ancient languages, irrespective of their obscurity. These translations remain but a pond's reflection of Xen in Eartherian, the text that will always be taught as long as our Species exists.

What pretentiousness you may ask would have led me even to consider an undertaking of this magnitude? I humbly submit this edition as my very best effort, without further ability to answer this question beyond my desire to have done so. I am contented with the final product, too.

I thank you for reading my translation on this occasion and hope it brings you lasting pleasure and satisfaction. If this is the case then I will have accomplished much more than satisfying my goal and, at the very least, contributed additional fodder for further students of the ancients. Let them reconcile the variations in choice of wording. It has been many generations since the last translation was completed. This is not to cast aspersions on earlier translations; I studied them all and was inspired by them toward this goal. Still, for households or students studying Ancient English, my work will serve as an additional choice on hand.

I have lent my efforts to bringing a different perspective to Xen, one that keeps with the spirit and intent of our beloved Story, but adds my knowledge of Ancient English, having studied and addressed this translation for a substantial portion of time.

For me this presentation completes a very long

standing wish and one that required significant maturity and discipline as you might well imagine. I didn't undertake this gargantuan effort without exposure. But if you must know: my credentials include careers in chemistry (I participated in synthesizing Altasone), architecture (I designed Loudon City's performing arts theater), manufacturing (my crew streamlined production of collecting arrays by 20%), engineering (we designed the light weight Thermous garments (keeping you warm when ambient temperatures are cold and (you get the picture))), and entertainment (I have performed dance, done illustrations, and written news stories for the general population on technical advances). I also have spent time in deep meditation and have seen many worlds prior to my marriage and many more since.

This translation of Xen into Ancient English has been a time to extend my mind, while I consider options and allow interests to congeal before striking out next. I'm considering ancient China, with specific reference to the dynastic rule vis-a-vis weapons of combustion. If you have had a particular interest or experience in either of these areas that you would like to pass on, please contact me via the publisher.

## Semifinal Note on this Edition

THERE WILL BE occasions when several words will be used to convey a concept, English being a salubrious abstraction with many pictures of the same subject being painted quite differently. If you find this irksome, go read Scor Tillum's translation with its (sorry S.T., but even your mother thought so) stilted prose. One word may be followed by many, many synonyms or other examples, which can be BORING, so use your finger, find the end of the sentence and go on. I have endeavored to produce as exact a translation as can be achieved with such limitations of Ancient English. If you don't want to read it this way or are offended by my translation, read the Original, another translation, or do one yourself. In other words, enjoy it or fuck** off; the choice is yours.

## Final Note on this Edition

THE READER WHO is not an advanced expert in Ancient English may find some of the words a bit troubling and others unsettling; thus, I encourage you to have access to a handy dictionary of this wonderful, albeit narrow, tongue. There are a few dozen or so words that have such a broad variety of interpretations that I have included them in a very brief Lexicon with their particular connotations as far as Xen is concerned. Use them cautiously in conjunction with other texts that you might try to decipher. These are so designated when first introduced with a double asterisk **, as in the preceding paragraph.

# Book 1 The Bet

IT WAS A dark and stormy night [DJS: as any reader of other English translations well knows, that's the best that English will do with this first line]. Actually it wasn't stormy in the traditional sense as will soon be apparent.

Wind was howling over Earth in a particular rampage. There had been quiet long enough! He was pissed. Glacial swirls of air buttressed escarpments, sculpting fronds of earth. Inspired, fueled, aided and abetted by bubbling lacunes of lava, Wind filled his quiver. The blasting of Earth there from, thrust from Heaven itself, came down with crackling stilettos.

Given sufficient time and no fuel or other technical constraints, it is said that a bulldozer can eventually move a mountain. For Wind, such a feat was but an eye blink, which is measurable and quite standardized.

Promontories were forged and then eradicated. Flatlands were relentlessly chiseled, eventually giving way to prepubescent invaginations of Earth. But cognizant of this being but a whisper of his power and always expelling detritus over his shoulder, Wind powered on. Furrows and slits developed in Earth; with continued poking, Wind bore down and ledges were constructed, allowing for panoramic observation of the evolving labor.

In his wake, valleys were cleaved, canyons were crafted, and caves sculpted.

But it wasn't always this way.

Forever oscillating since his birth, Wind could only tangentially recall his origin. Earth had already been present for many Rotations** he, in time, came to realize.

Sentience really came with perceptions of air tickling over the hellish terrain. Hellishly hot that is, no other visions of the land beyond purgatory being intended, the word overstepping its bounds.

The whole Earth was hell, it seemed to Wind. No matter where those early tufts of air traveled, molten rock greeted him with a searing smack. Polar regions were minimally more hospitable, sending Wind oscillating in the opposite direction with a fraternal spank by comparison to the impaling he encountered in the tropics. Aye Carrumba!

Wind pogoed all over Earth at one time or another, dwelling in circular serpentine gales at times, moving horizontally with little alacrity. Other periods caught Wind prancing from Point A to Point B, and still in others Wind catapulted forth in a parabolic trajectory with force so great that a little part of him made it to the troposphere and Beyond.

But with virtually unlimited latitude, in this setting at least, there was a cost. From breezes to land based hurricanes, from tornados to terrestrial doldrums, Wind had been everywhere and done everything he could and quite redundantly at that.

After seemingly uncountable Rotations, Wind had begun to be a little testy. Actually, they are countable, being a billion, plus or minus, for the sake of simplicity and in order to define our terms, say an even billion; a seemingly very large number until one considers a stack of one billion dollar** bills. These would extend far less than seventy-five miles, since they are as thin as they are worthless; eventually coming to be known as the skunk** (now after all, one North American currency unit is known as a loony, another is a peso which is inherently a joke that no animal could possibly represent other than perhaps the hyena and he wouldn't be laughing), previous monikers having been the greenback, buck, etc, fortuitously rhyming with funk which is what holders of dollars were in as the skunk's true value became clear. That's the beauty of a fiat currency; when it becomes worthless, it doesn't cost a whole lot more just to print a new one. Such is the cost of government by democracy rather than through liberty.

Anyway, Wind sure has had his fun with paper currency, but that's another story.

Back in those adolescent days, when Earth was a young adult, Wind was frolicking from one set of coordinates to gamboling over another. Always onward, sometimes back, resting at times, energy from Earth's heat ejaculated through his arteries.

Wind blew to the Four Corners. Earth began to cool.

The latter wasn't really obvious to Wind at first. We are talking about expansive Rotations here. But then during one revolution of anything you wish to imagine in terms of stellar time short of the whole enchilada's, the Universe's, beginning and end (look again, DURING, not after), Wind became convinced.

It was over the poles. No longer belted with a spank on the way back, Wind was now christened on his rump with but a potch**. Around Earth's bloated belly, the hellfire was not perceptibly diminished.

Still, this was a first step toward his union with Earth, Wind eventually surmised. Bored with his transmutations and with Earth cooling, Wind decided he would begin to have some fun.

And so Wind began sculpting Earth. Little improvisations at first, fluting over incipient wells of raw material.

But after sufficient time and with an active imagination, Wind took on epochal projects, which is where the story started, more or less.

That night in question really wasn't any different from eons of others, the storm of that night that is. Which was part of the problem.

By this time Wind and Earth had bonded. Each respected the other and Earth reveled in the attention Wind showed her. She quivered under his caress at times and bucked to his massage at others; becoming more malleable with each cycle (measurable, even if not with current instruments), she surrendered herself completely to his entreaties and direction.

She embraced him and he loved her.

But like in all relationships, there were vicissitudes that did not necessarily divide them, but challenged their patience and understanding.

The storm in question was a night where compassion had been rendered extinct. Vacillating in force, depth and duration, Wind had been piercing Earth's flesh for seemingly, in fact, ages. Mountains had been formed, reaching such heights that even Wind felt rarified at their zenith. Mounds of Earth so numerous and heaping caused dimpling of other landscapes. Geologic formations of all descriptions had been contrived by Wind upon the bosom of Earth.

SSDD**. Wind was exasperated. He was happy with Earth of course; they were friends and always would be. But this epochal ennui had weighed on Wind, causing him to writhe upon Earth with fury.

Earth absorbed it all with great beneficence and her reserves were near infinite. But she knew how Wind pained.

And so during all their bluster one night, with Earth having cooled to just the right degree (literally), Wind and Earth cavorted into an orgasmic extravaganza, and Water was born upon Earth.

Wind jubilantly bore the little vapor upon his brow and together they journeyed over Earth. Adventures galore awaited them over time. Water coalesced into pools scooped out of Earth by her companion, Wind; these evolved into lakes and eventually the rivers and oceans, Earth sharing her bounty with Water.

And from Water sprang forth life itself. Eventually all the creatures of Earth came to exist, single and multicellular, plant and animal, instinctive and conniving.

Each fought among various others like and dissimilar to themselves for survival; each was another's bread and butter, each was another's executioner in the abattoir of life itself.

Still there was an equilibrium overall; everything had its time of maximal numbers, waxing and waning, but not to nadirs of such depths that a Species was totally annihilated except through climactic changes of geologic proportions; after all, nothing is immortal. Otherwise, all thrived, even if individuals expired, again which is expected over time. No reason to bemoan the inevitable.

Wind and Water and Earth nurtured their offspring and played with them. Encouragement with challenge were the buzzwords.

Wind spread the bounty of pollen and the subsequent seedlings brought forth from fertilization. Water challenged spawning so that only the most determined to procreate would survive. Eggs were laid of all colors, textures, and sizes. With Wind's watchful eye, just enough, at the right temperature and in the right direction, they would be undisturbed until hatching, launching another delightful if not voracious organism upon Earth, their corporeal matrix being lent substance by Water herself.

Both Wind and Water, who was rapidly catching up to her friend's abilities, each had their own favorite creatures. Birds (and others) would flit ultimately from one outpost of Earth to another but graze through the Heavens, propelled by Wind's grace and vector. Water became the domicile for both aerobes as well as numbers of anaerobes. There were babies as well as the young whose lives would transmigrate Earth and Water, and a near infinite variety (and number) of bugs.

Water sustained the land-based who, from their inception, only borrowed the molecules that formed their basis, always recycling the Hs and Os not literally passed on to other structures. Thirsts at all levels were satiated by Water's cornucopia and Wind and Earth made sure that Water herself was appropriately renewed and healthy.

Earth took it all in stride; the good, the bad; the life and death. Even Fire**, when it came.

Fire was an expeditious tool for Earth, a scalpel for razing blemishes, allowing for a face lift on virgin terrain. Sometimes, after long periods of rhythmic borborygmi** under her crust, eructations of hell would follow. Such fire-works were always guaranteed to whisk Wind into high gear and put Water on the defensive.

For Fire once having materialized acted not against its nature, desecrating everything within grasp, taking no prisoners and leaving survivors who would rather not have been so designated.

The suffering made Water sigh, attempting to minimize Fire's damage. But this wasn't always simple, given Wind's propensity to become psychotic, mesmerized by Fire's apparent magic and power. After all, Fire could cause greater havoc in a much shorter time than Wind, even with considerable muster and predisposition. Accordingly, like a jealous understudy, Wind would get into the Act, fawning for attention from Fire, which had been pandering all along. And Fire used Wind's temerity to augment its own path and survival, gobbling up all homes and creatures within its tentacles. An ephemeral hydra that exists in warmth and sight, smell and sound, but which cannot be grasped. The horror and disgust were self evident.

Eventually, Water would get the upper hand, with or without Wind's having abandoned his castles in the sky, and Fire would be extinguished—once again. Water appreciated Wind's help when offered and didn't hold a grudge when Wind was consumed with hegemonic delusions.

They both realized that some Fire was occasionally brought forth by their very union, in a theatrical tête-à-tête that was markedly distinguished from the dark and stormy night with which the story began. Thus, there were no innocents, just victims, the deranged, and the heroes.

Earth's marquee boasted an ongoing melee of adventure, with one act sure to follow another, variably headlined by solos or duets or even the complete trio, as ticket sales and demand warranted. Displays of flora, bedecked by dew the shape of diamonds and pearls, announced the changing program and Stars.

There were sonnets, conflagrations, ballets and campy tea parties followed by cacophonous maelstroms. Coronations, funerals, costume balls, minuets, fugues, slapstick, and twists, all had a venue in Earth's theater. There were times when Water was the ringleader, cleansing Earth in a furious wiping of the slate, the left over sets from each Act not always meticulously recycled, the landscape having become an asylum of props. But at least Wind and Water were exculpated from the most dastardly scenes, during which Fire was not to be outdone.

Acknowledged by all players to be Earth's quintessential progeny was, observably, Homo sapiens. Mankind had after all eventually designed immolating machines of varying degrees of complexity. But like some beasts brought into their household, Fire could never be entirely domesticated and there were times when Mankind was burned badly, literally.

Serenity was the outfit of the day when Wind caught up with Water over a bucolic lake; Wind had been so quiet on his approach. But no matter how gently this zephyr exhaled, his very proximity excited her when she lay upon Earth, ripe of latitude, the tinkling over her surface sending her in a coy retreat. Thus, Wind was never able to completely look his ward in the eye. It was only at her surface that Water and Wind could meld, overpowering with their zeal the physics that divided their domains; where they could exchange molecular heirlooms, replenish supplies of rare earths, metals, salts, and gases, each offering dowry and legacy; where they could for at least fractions of atomic time, become one.

Bliss at this level was divine but Wind longed for antithetical stimulation as well. He desired just to gaze upon those limpid bodies that he thought pocked Earth, from the puddles to the oceans themselves, without setting them into motion and making his view of Water tainted. When Water was in his domain, variably as snow, rain, hail, sleet, he could gape at all her strutting poses from multiple angles and for as long as he cared and at any magnification or perspective. When Water covered the polar regions or others far affected by the cold, Wind could easily get up close and personal with her; she was solid like Earth only more fragile. But in those environments she succumbed to the somniferous spell of the local gastronomy, being too drunk and dreamy to be any fun.

They would still interact at the Surface but for Wind that was about as exhilarating as sex in a bad marriage**.

Wind respected Water's sabbaticals and rest in the frigid environs. Goodness knows she gave him a wide berth. And when Water was in the tropics, her sheer outfits and peppery disposition had been known to send Wind into convulsions of lust. After those unions, Wind was languorous and Water smiling. For Wind, the pump was so good that he forgot, or at least didn't care, about his mate's akathisia** under his gaze.

It had been some time since they had tangoed along the equator.

Did Wind say pocked earlier, this verb connecting Water upon Earth? Yes, but he didn't really mean anything pejorative and he had begun to notice that that wouldn't have been an apt description anyway. Earth wasn't actually pocked by Water at all. Earth was, by this time, virtually enveloped by Water.

Look at how intimate Water and Earth have become, he thought. Over time Earth had gladly given up huge portions of her surface to Water's ebullience. In fact, Earth had snuggled under Water's expansive comforter, peeking out variably here and there. Here was true symbiosis.

This somehow irritated Wind when his zephyrus envoy approached the lake that day. He had been attracted to her because of her cheesecake posture. The Sun had been crisply frying the Heavens and the clouds had been boiled out of their ethereal cauldron. Water just wanted to revel in the warmth to the maximum her pores would allow. Not being inhibited, she spread herself to an acme of surface area over that portion of Earth. This initially titillated Wind, seeing Water so garishly exposed, flush against Earth—*femina a femina*. But then he thought again about how close Earth and Water had become. He wasn't particularly jealous, but it irked him. After all, they were a threesome; everyone hated Fire.

While this disenchantment wouldn't cause any lasting rift in their friendship, it did slow the old anemometer down and Wind became cranky.

"You're looking quite fetching," Wind palpably panted to Water, barely able to keep it in his pants.

"Oh, Wind," she cooed, "I felt your approach." Wind was pleased with this acknowledgement of his tepid fingering, but his petals began to wilt by what followed. "The Sun feels soooo good, electrifying my surface." Her words pricked him even while she purred into his ear.

Sit still for christsake, he thought, let me get a look at you. You're pulsating. Stop it. With a smidgeon of desperation, he thought about how her movement was the result of the Sun's "electrification," when in fact it was his own observation of Water that cursed his voyeuristic desires.

But at that very moment he also sensed a problem in the Forest. With Wind ubiquitously gallivanting over Earth, he was omnipotent to all that went on in his domain, from the fracases to the miracles.

So off he raced, sweetly embracing Water as he departed, though she seemed not to notice. She was mesmerized by the Sun, like the groupie flowers that enlaced her banks. Whatever, he thought, scurrying into the Forest, I think Water is getting a bit stuck up.

In the Forest were several human children who had gotten lost from their families; the little ones were crying for their mommies and even the older ones were becoming a bit panicky. When all of a sudden a great gust of Wind came right in their faces, causing them to blink and turn and run in the opposite direction, then to the right and now left down a different path. They hadn't gone too far when Wind began to dissipate and they stood still for a few moments, catching their breath. Wind then rustled through the shrubs and bushes in front of the children, removing some vegetation that had recently engulfed the stones that marked their way home; the tears turned from despair and foreboding to excitement and relief as they chopped out full bore in a race toward the village, gentle taunts rapidly replacing the earlier camaraderie.

"Mankind is such a funny fuck, don't you think?" he asked rhetorically to Water upon returning to the lake. He had wasted no time redirecting his attention to his earlier passion.

"Mankind is such a funny duck?" she whispered, obviously misunderstanding his query, dozing under the Sun's penumbra.

"Funny FUCK!" he roared. And then becoming more civil, "Why would I want to equate humans with a Water fowl that forms a queue before any action is taken?"

Blinking from her reverie, Water sputtered, "Funny fuck? Whatever do you mean?" Now he had her attention. And without missing a beat she added, "Your help of those human children was quite magnanimous."

"Eleemosynary," he mumbled, almost embarrassed. Like Wind, Water through her tributaries, was privy to all events on Earth. She knew Wind, despite his obvious bluster, was committed to equanimity on their turf above all else. Which is why she didn't understand his question.

"Funny fuck, funny fuck!" he repeated. "You saw what happened, didn't you. Weren't you paying attention? Or was your butt too raw from the Sun's tanning?"

Now perceiving his obvious need for attention, Water withdrew from some of the Sun's exposure, assuming a more demure stance. Which at once made Wind more buggy, given his lascivious nature, now more stoked with the tease.

But he quickly got over these palpitations, being serious with her. At least as much as he could be, she thought.

"I think humans are such funny fucks," he said again. Wherever is this going to go? Water thought. And Wind continued, "They vacillate so readily from one extreme to another. One moment they are forlorn; the next they are challenging each other. Their vagaries I find disconcerting."

I wonder where humans learned that from, she presciently thought to herself, rather than saying this aloud. She still wasn't sure where this conversation was heading. He was rarely so obtuse, but she let him continue.

"In the process of uncovering those stones, a bird's nest was toppled onto the ground. I'm sure you watched those children whose stomachs had been taut with fear greedily grab up the eggs for a future dinner, whooping over their good luck. The bird's misfortune."

"Yes, of course I did," she sighed. "We know that is the way of our world. So what?"

"Yes, all creatures strive for survival," he agreed. "But Mankind has harnessed if not mastered Fire among his many accomplishments. And I have seen how they look at their mates and their peers, with eyes belying their perfection at refracting images."

Water had noted these behaviors among humans as well although her interpretation was more benign. "Humans live in small enclaves, hunting other beasts and gathering flora for sustenance. They are born, they grow, they mate, they die. They become one with Earth again and their molecular remains are brought asunder by both you and me. On a clock with celestial divisions, even we and our Mother Earth are not immortal."

"YYW**," he monotoned, not having the appetite for a jumbo sized portion of her canned platitudes. "I think Mankind will be unlike any of our other creatures in sufficient time," Wind puffed worriedly. And then with cyclonic vehemence, he added, "he will try to take on even us!"

"As if**! What are you chattering about?" She was now becoming a bit concerned although she wondered if this wasn't one of Wind's elaborate games and she was just being slow to take the bait.

"Here and now I predict that Mankind will destroy himself. And possibly take us with him, intentionally or without malice. It won't matter."

"Not a chance," Water shot back, with more than a little defensiveness given life's origins. "Mankind's soul is inherently good. But I agree it might need tweaking periodically, just as our shenanigans have affected all creatures throughout all time." She smiled, but was somewhat bored over the insipid nature of the debate. She saw that Wind was becoming more melancholy as he appeared deep in thought. He was no longer tapping on branches in the Forest in fits of nervous tension, now barely perceptible.

She knew just the answer. A challenge. A bet. "I'm willing to bet," she began lyrically, almost mockingly, "that Mankind will turn out just fine."

"And you will accomplish this, no doubt?" he entreated with gathering gusts. "I have been with Earth many more Rotations than you, lover. I do not think you have the power. There is a conceit in your proposition. I could easily destroy Mankind."

"But you won't certainly. I know you better than that," Water admonished. "I too could annihilate Mankind if that was my goal. You know that I have become powerful enough. But I adore all our creatures, especially Mankind; when extinction of a Species occurs, it is not to be our doing. And I do not fear Mankind."

"I hardly have trepidation where Mankind is concerned," Wind effused, bucking up more from his previous tepid demeanor. "And I witness your awesome force, albeit secondary to mine."

Whatever, she thought; she could always count on Wind's hubris and wasn't going to get suckered into another tits versus dick comparison, at least not at that raunchy level.

"But what is this Bet you began to proffer?" Wind's tempo was beginning to increase in cadence.

"Just what I said," Water countered, volleying little tempests of steam into Wind's puss. "I am willing to bet that Mankind will evolve, albeit with waxing and waning fortitude, ultimately becoming a little brother (read sister she thought) of ours."

"With each of us continuing to have our fun, just as we always have with Earth?" he asked.

"Yes, of course. I'm not about to give up our paddy cake and other frivolities any more than the nurturing and lessons required by our progeny."

"I'm not about to change my direction," Wind clucked, which naturally was a diminutive to which he couldn't adhere. But he liked the idea of a little brother; the porism had him streaking through the skies.

By now the Sun was beginning her sleep on that side of Earth, wiggling her corona under the horizon's mantle. Wind and Water were becoming weary, but the clarification of the Bet was not complete.

"The bottom line," began Water prosaically. "We each go about our business as usual; help some, exterminate others, all in the name of fun and Earth's best interest. Neither of us can definitively cause upheaval of such magnitude that Mankind is either saved or lost. By this I mean we cannot decimate one or more Species so that our point of view is ultimately proven."

"And if I win?" Wind gustily queried. "If Mankind evolves to a position of extinguishing himself from Earth's palate, what is my reward?" They had participated in speculations before, each fading the other, but the spoils were relatively trivial.

"If you win, the change to the ecosystem will be catastrophic anyway," Water sardonically lapped; exhausted now, her patience was evaporating. "I will endeavor to grant you that for which you so lustily yearn. I will find it in my nature to exist in staid form for your visual pleasure."

"And if I am wrong?" Wind barely fluttered, for he too was becoming exhausted. He sheepishly thought of the devastating repercussions if he was right, but he didn't like being wrong.

"If I win, I'll have the satisfaction of having kicked your ass! Which is always enough of a reward to me," Water languidly lipped her embankments.

"As if!" Wind chortled; here was a safe wager, with great upside potential and minimal risk. "Your lethargy is murkily affecting your judgment, dearest Water. Nevertheless, in the spirit of our long companionship, I accept your challenge and agree to your terms." And with that, not even waiting for any further rejoinder from Water, he catapulted across the Forest, looking for other adventure.

Water had no witty riposte anyway. She just winked to the creatures around her, and nuzzled against Earth.

# Book 2 Scientist I

## Day 1

AH THE SUBWAY, you think, nostalgically. The first you ever rode was in New York City, visiting with a friend from college. What better place to start in terms of underground trains but with one that is now over a hundred years old? Subways provide transportation only in large metropolitan areas, where you have had many great experiences and, fortunately, few bad ones.

This station is practically immaculate. No piss or shit** on the stairs, a minimal number of sleeping bums who don't hastle you, no vomit or spilled drinks. This one is crowded and not well laid out. You find the ticket booth.

"How much, please, to go to Constantinople stop," you ask. "And which train is it?" No answer. While threading a $5.00 bill through the opening at the bottom of the bullet proof glass, you say again, much louder, "Constantinople stop! Which train?"

As you take your ticket, you think, rude, deaf token agents behind glass that distorts their features; no one alive could be that ugly; they're all the same in that regard. What this subway doesn't have in gastrointestinal goings or comings, it makes up for in visual eyesores.

First there is the graffiti. What kind of an asshole wastes money and time vandalizing otherwise decently painted municipal property? You know the answers indeed —asserting independence and impressing peers, mooning authority, the thrill of the risk of being caught, the minimal penalty if caught, etc, etc. Wow, you're sooo impressed by their statements; don't you wish you had their *cojones*? You certainly wish you had their time to kill.

The few benches are all taken. You wouldn't sit, even if one was available. You'd rather stand in a situation like this, allowing for shifting of your body and head as you do what you are so trained to do, observe and reflect. Your bag would be between your legs if it wasn't so wide; thus you place it near your right leg, the outside of your shoe just touching it.

The other visually disturbing aspect of this subway system in general and the stop in particular is the patrons themselves. While the images threaten to scramble your rods and cones, they are also quite intellectually satisfying in terms of their variety and scope, their diversity and banality, a marked contrast to the typical scumbag** that you encounter back home.

Naturally there are plenty of niggers**; mostly fat, some thin, generally skuzzy like you remember; city niggers have more airs than the country niggers (probably on account that they can at least read and write at the 6th grade level), but a nigger is a nigger. With caricatured clothing of type, color, texture, pattern, size, style and even how it is worn, not an option is missed for making them out as anything but niggers. Even from orbit their fashion statements become hyperbole of vomitious taste. Could they all be in costume on their way to their work on the stage or perhaps they are all going to the same costume ball? Neither of those could really be possible because what other role could they be playing in that hysterical garb other than nigger? Don't they get it you think? But that one is easy as well, clothing being a microcosm of the overall problem, which you don't feel like mentally debating.

You hear the train coming in the distance and you adjust your position on the platform. You're the only one who moves; everyone else is essentially frozen in space. You wonder whether the intransigence of city dwellers like these is from arrogance; or are they just fucking deaf from the subway and all the other noise. On the corner above there are scores of people walking and talking, with their periodic but collective eructations and flatulence; hundreds of wheezing motor vehicle engines along with their horns and screeching tires, machinery of construction, jackhammers for deconstruction, traffic whistles, jets overhead, boom boxes, and the subway below. The din would be maddening if you had to listen to it daily. You see the front lamp approach.

Several niggers quit slouching and meander to the platform. No they're not drunk, you guess, given their conversation; stoned, probably. If one is a nigger, he has to get high; how else can he or she cope with being a nigger?

"Skin 'em and use 'em for wet suits," you recall reading as a child in the bathroom of the local drug store. You and your brother used to ride your bikes there for candy, comic books, soft drinks**, records and just something to do; there were no niggers in your neighborhood, not a one. Stupid, shiftless, irresponsible, over sexed, lazy, liars, thieves; any nigger with more than subhuman intelligence must have at least some white blood you've read. You don't actually believe that of course, but you know those who do.

The doors open, the car pukes its human detritus (incoming you think), more scumbags and you get on. You stand, clutching your suitcase handle, while you look for a seat.

Many of them are taken by one nigger or another. As the train screeches forward, causing you momentary deafness, you catapult to a vacant one that isn't sporting the need for a wet cloth and bleach. Sitting and expressionless, you think about the bureaucracy of government moving from three part forms completed on a typewriter in triplicate, with whiteout supplies on back order, to high speed wireless. Such technologic feats occur when a nigger applies for Medicaid and food stamps while sitting at home after her fender bender; you know, the one where her car was struck by another that ran a stop sign; she didn't go to the hospital at that time, just feeling a little shaken; she drove her car home; several weeks later she began having pain in her head and diffusely in her body; she is having trouble walking, she can't sit still, her bladder and bowels don't work now, she is dizzy, falling out, having seizures, her arms and legs are numb and burn, she can't sleep, things don't taste right, she is gaining weight, she can't breathe since she started smoking again, and she can't sexually climax anymore. She was just about to start looking for a job when the accident occurred and she certainly can't work now. Voila! Give me, get me, bring me, buy me, more, more more. And the case might not be settled for years. So now, she has to spend her time sleeping late since she can't sleep at night, doing crafts at home as best she can, helping at the Church**, and doing lots of fucking in case her orgasms come back; it wouldn't be fair to miss even one because of that nasty, stupid, inconsiderate, irresponsible other driver; at least that's what her disabled fiancé tells her.

You watch them walk. Why can't they walk right either? Why do they have to shuffle, which reminds you of the joke about their knuckles scraping the ground. Which then reminds you of the one about inflate to 40 psi tattooed on the inside of their lips. Which then reminds you of the watchful admonition in any situation where a joint is being passed around, "don't nigger lip it."

You tend to stare into oblivion, glancing at those sitting and standing. The only people you get up for are pregnant women, women with small children and old ladies; othe-rwise, fuck 'em; you got there first.

Look at that nigger sitting across from you, you think. Leather everything; hat, vest, jacket, pants, tie. Goddamn, is that shirt of his leather too? What about his fucking underwear and socks you wonder? And get this, he's got on SNEAKERS, which are WHITE. What a NIGGER, your brain screams inside your head. If black is beautiful, to use the saw that is not only old but trite, then you shat a major masterpiece this morning.

And the mofo** next to him, just a little patch of fuzz below his lower lip and on his chin; what's the matter nigger? Massah take the razor back before you finish every day at the exact same time? Plan ahead for christsake. Geez, what a nigger.

You check out the female niggers. There are a litany on the train; they are a gaggle of jewelry, big nails, expensive hair, garish outfits, obnoxious cell phones, and handbags big enough to hide just about any stolen item short of two watermelons simultaneously (she could get two in there, you think, but she'd have to remove the fifth as well as all the pill bottles, sacrosanct items even when compared to a second watermelon). What is with this blond hair on the one in the leopard outfit? A sight that never ceases to leave you incredulous; how can that nigger think she looks good in blond hair unless she is comparing herself to her even more preposterous sister with the red hair? Sister your ass; they're as related as your beagle is to the poodle next door.

You have a sip of your coffee. If you're going to pay for something to drink, it is damn well going to have something in it. You'll be damned if you're going to pay one skunk to drink Water allegedly without something in it. If the city or county Water is that bad, why are we still paying for it? And if there is a cover up, then your heirs will have a cause of action and a chance to join the great lottery of our tort justice system. So you're really thinking about your children; after all, your greatest legacy to them was assuring them that it was OK to drink soda** in the mornings. The breeze from the air conditioning is at least working, you think; temperature wise, it is quite pleasant.

Your gaze gradually skips down the rest of the car; you're sitting near the center, adjacent to a door, your favorite spot. The route map is also best visualized from this location, so you know you can count off the stations before yours.

Niggers, jigaboos, coons, darkies, spear chuckers, jabos, picaninnies, spades, jungle bunnies, porch monkeys, reindeer, they're all the same. But they're no better or worse than the spics, wops, chinks, nips, pollocks, wet backs, kikes, peckerwoods, crackers, lymies, canucks, and sand niggers also taking up space in this train. You don't see any Indians; you've got lots of those back home.

You think about the Chicanos, or Mexican Americans, or whatever their current preferred label. What a bunch of fucking beaners; they're so stupid they have to begin a question with a question mark so they'll know it is coming; same thing with the exclamation point; in other words, get ready, something big is coming. At least they work. Like the saying goes: every white boy should have a nigger to do his work and every nigger should have a Mexican to do HIS work.

One stop, not yours. People on, people off. There is a nigger talking to himself; that's always a red flag that you might want to relocate as soon as possible. Not much worse than a crazy nigger.

The station is left behind. Everybody settles in again. Some are reading (fancy that); many are listening to music louder than legally allowed (surprise). There are no guards on this car. Most are just sitting there, taking up space, useful oxygen, food and liquor; what a waste of good resources. There aren't enough trees to hang them all on, you think.

You look at their hands, well at least the women's. Lots of cheap, discount store rings; you doubt any of them are wedding rings. Most of them don't get married. God forbid. And when they do and it doesn't work out, they just stay long term separated, each too cheap to pay for a divorce. Not that that stops them from shacking up with whoever is more pathetic than themselves. And while there is plenty of money for booze, drugs and cigarettes, there's never enough left over for any medications let alone birth control. So their numbers go up exponentially and you wonder why you are having to pay for millions of other people's children; yours were expensive enough for Christ-sake; that's why you weaned them early on from dairy to soft drinks.

You've thought this one through before; everyone's allowed to fuck up once. Ok, they didn't understand that sexual intercourse can result in children—here's the free ride; tell the name of the father, the state will verify this by DNA, and he can have some of his wages garnished for the next eighteen years; the state will find work for him to do; if they don't know the father or refuse to name him, which is their RIGHT, no problem but no more support beyond this one. The second out of wedlock child will be given up for adoption and they will be sterilized. Seems pretty straight forward to you; you're not asking for help raising your children.

Your stop is here. The train heaves and lurches. You disembark without incident, none too soon since the talking nigger comes close and you see he's packing a Bible. The circus moves down the track with measured monotony.

You walk the block and a half to your hotel. The lobby downstairs is nice, but nothing special. Now the angel behind the desk, she's another thing. What a piece of ass! "Hi, I have a reservation," you say, "Seneschal, Pawkey Seneschal." You pull out your reservation confirmation and a credit card. She couldn't possibly see the lust in your mind, you think, or she'd slap you for sure. Yeah, women are making gains you think; but to answer the age old question, you'd fuck her.

You keep walking and walking to find your room; it's not the last one but damn near you think. It's a damn good thing your suitcase has wheels; that motherfucker is heavy. Off with your shoes, the suitcase plops on the bed, looking nine months pregnant, and you haven't even gotten anything yet. Shit.

The conference begins in the morning; you look forward to this every year. On first impression, the room seems fine. Whoa, how wrong you can be with initial assessments. Let's see. In this wonderful city, you have a view of rooms across from you in another wing; fabulous. With a favorable Wind you think, you could probably piss into one of them, the alley separating the corridors is that narrow. The bed feels comfortable. The place is hot; you turn the fan on high and the thermostat to maximal cold. There is a huge air vent in the hall next to your room that sucks the air with a sound typically heard in the wake of small airplanes; yep, you've got a quiet room. At least you won't have to worry about your television being too loud. WHAT! No movie channels? Not even a FUCKING PAY

FOR VIEW. You guess 200 skunks doesn't buy what it used to; there's a surprise. Goddamnit. This is the same shit you can watch at home; no, belay that; they have LESS fucking channels than you do at home.

Christ on a crutch. Whatever, you think. You're not here for the television anyway. You call home briefly to have them call back since it is way too expensive to use direct dial from the hotel. The bitch wife never calls you back. You call her again, same thing.

So you hook up your PCD** to the local outlet. You had verified the availability of a local access number prior to the trip; while you are away, that becomes the default, your home local number being listed as an alternative. No problem. Wonder of wonders! It actually works. The first time. You check your stuff—messages from your office, businesses, and other offshoots of interest. Copasetic.

You go downstairs, get directions to the nearest little store so you can get some drinks to take back upstairs. You apparently misunderstand the directions and go entirely around the block to end up about twenty feet from where you came out of the hotel if you had just gone in the right direction.

Goddamn is this town full of niggers, or what? They're everywhere, you think; maybe there's a special nigger convention at your hotel. Certainly the number at your conference is at most one percent if the past is any prelude. You figure out there was a concert nearby by listening to conversations as you slowly but deliberately walk and observe the fans toting band paraphernalia.

You get back to your room, without incident. As you sit there, the chair's not bad, flipping the channels, the remote stops working. What the hell! You fuck with the batteries; it starts working again.

A show depicting life in a southern family comes on; southern hospitality is a bigger oxymoron than honest lawyer, you think; and the only thing honest about the average barrister is that he honestly wants his fee. And you start thinking again. Back home you've got maybe six traffic lights, probably not more; you'd bet a dollar about that, this being a safe bet since a dollar has become so worthless these days.

Back home you've got lots of niggers too. They're stupider and fatter than their city counterparts, but otherwise not appreciably different. They're treated just fine in your county. There is no discrimination. All the restaurants back home serve niggers of course; you just have to specify how you like them prepared. Back home most everyone you know has nothing against niggers either, figuring that every family should have one, preferably two for breeding purposes.

The only thing worse than your basic, garden variety nigger is a nigger "leader." Not that you have anything against their rabble rousing; that's fine. What you can't stand is their obvious hypocrisy, their primary goal being to "represent" their downtrodden, while living a luxurious life style and typically fucking everything with a skirt (...or God help us).

So the self appointed HNICs**, manifestly more heinous because of the alleged faith that they swaddle around their loins and with dudgeon to spare, are worse; but more despicable still are the PWTs**. They are just like the niggers except more shameful because they don't have the burden of black skin; you have listened to them dump on their black brethren. Criminy jickets! Where else but your home town and thousands like it across the country would you read the headline in the biweekly newsrepeater, "Gunfire outs T ball game?" Or an obituary that pays tribute to the deceased's pets, including the fish, by name? Or where a thank you is sent into the newspaper after a bad cyclone, expressing appreciation for the multiple chicken plates; or where the physicians are addressed as "mister" but the PAs are referred to as "doctor;" or where a home cleaning operation goes by the hook, "Sisters in Christ?" The only thing more infinite than the number of hypocritical preachers, which transcends all colors of skin, (send two box top panels and one dollar and a diploma of faith is available when they get the calling, (from whom you wonder)) is the axiomatically larger infinite value representing their congregants. Through selfless pedagogic toils, they instruct the young parishioners, often quite ecumenical with regard to both sexes, in giving proper homage to their staffs, thus assuring themselves ongoing religious experiences with which they can inspire their sheep.

The PWTs are, with few exceptions, morbidly obese by any set of criteria other than extra-terrestrial blimps; and they want to know why their knees and other joints hurt. How 'bout losing a few hundred pounds, you think; they just might feel better. There are the PWT shit cans; these are the ones you'd have to dip before you would touch them without gloves; others come along without shoes, "'cause their feet hurt!" Many got as far as elementary school; you remember one who said he didn't go farther than first grade. He wasn't a tard** either. You think about this and how this could have happened. Yeah, sometime during that first year of school, he went home one day and said Ma, Pa, I don't feel like going back and they must have said OK.

You think again, at least the PWTs don't have the excuse of living with integument enriched with melanin. Their haughtiness towards the niggers is not to be believed. This while the men have a gut and a half and the women have cooter** rolls of blubber so massive that the local dancing hippos would feel svelte enough to attempt the Can-Can. How in the hell do they find it to wipe? Wait, what's that smell you think? And how in the hell do they find it for fucking? Now there is a mystery; neither the women nor the men have been able to see their feet when standing up for years; if they couldn't slip their shoes on and feel them on their feet, they'd have to go barefoot. Yet they all have children. Some up to ten head or more. God you think, are people ever fecund, or what. Clearly we're designed to breed.

Back home you know of grandparents in their thirties. Their thirties for christsake; which means that they become great grandparents by their fifties and so on. You've done the math. You've seen the multiple generations. They are funeralized, not buried, when they die. They're kept at home long after it is in their best interest by greedy, self interested relatives who usurp their welfare checks each month.

And they speak a different language certainly, one that you learned in an earlier career in the insurance industry. They don't pass out, they "fall out." They don't have spinal meningitis; they have the "screaming mighty Jesus." When they go blind, they "can still see." Any plural quantity cannot be parsed more definitively than "right much," which can also be used for the degree of a subjective problem. They don't get uterine fibroids; they get "fireballs of the Eucharist." Food doesn't go down their esophagus; it goes down their "sockapus." They don't have a hiatal hernia; they have a "hiatyherny." Thankfully, those of the female persuasion don't suffer from pelvic inflammatory disease, but they can contract "pussy in distress." They don't get MRIs; they get MIRs. They get "skrokes," not strokes. Their whole circulatory system consists of veins, on both sides of the heart. Their blood pressure is massively high but they "only had a little pork over the weekend." When confronted in a compromising posture, they need "ocky-gin;" last time you checked, you need the same, regardless of your position. And when they call for help, they dial 919 or 191 or 119 and then get angry when no other idiot picks up. Even the fucking teachers can't speak English. And not surprisingly, fiancé has come to mean the person they're currently fucking, nothing else.

You turn off the television in an attempt to settle down, getting undressed as much as you normally do and get into bed. Despite the noise from the fan in the hallway, you turn the noise maker on, providing additional white background sounds that are pleasingly familiar to your ear. Tomorrow is going to be a big day in terms of the conference. It's the first day and these go from early morning to dark. Still, you're too wound up to sleep. At least you don't have anything this year to present.

You think as you lie there. Now you know you don't have a prejudiced bone in your body; that's the scary part.

You were raised in a home where colored people did some occasional cleaning or other light work; ditto with your grandparents' schvartzes. The N word was never used except by you and your brother when whispering a joke heard at school. You recall your brother saying the N word in front of your grandmother one time. It was one time only since she leapt off her divan like a spring had just broken and was literally screwing with her asshole, yelling "look here" as she pulled the ping-pong paddle from the waist holster she wore whenever you were visiting; you don't recall seeing her move so fast. Unable to help it, you chuckle out loud, as you mentally image behind your closed eyes the rapture of her intent: if flints were hidden in her bra, the gyrations of her boobs would have caused the whole place to go up in flames and you wouldn't be here now staying in this shitty hotel tonight. You never said the N word in front of her after seeing your brother unsuccessfully try to outrun her and hide. Your brother, who is a few years older, was always pretty good about fucking up and you learned from his mistakes. An uncle once praised him for helping you, saying something like, '[he] needed to teach you everything he knew;' you recall thinking that wasn't going to take long.

You used to think your grandmother's ping-pong paddle was standard issue to all new grandmothers until you told a friend about the incident and he invited you to his grandmother's house, assuring you that his didn't carry any such thing. He was right you found out; she carried a red club made of plastic or rubber, maybe both, that clipped to her pants or dress. You couldn't tell from the distance you were content to maintain from her and he couldn't remember. He said he thought the ping-pong paddle would probably be better since an adult would be less inclined to smack you on the head with it versus going for a couple whacks with the club.

But as far as the N word was concerned, your first memory was eeny, meeny, miney, moe... you taught your children [...tiger...].

You fall asleep. Your dreams are vivid and interminable

you feel, but you don't sleep well. The only thing you recall is one particular set of unholy trinities** .

## Day 2

FOR LUNCH YOU head down the street from the hotel, which is on a main thoroughfare. You're hungry and look at the options for basic burgers, cheap, filling, and hopefully not too salty for your taste; ditto for the fries. You had nothing for breakfast as usual, other than a mug of coffee in one hand and in the other a bottle of Water that is carbonated and sweet but not fattening (of course). Now that's how to start the morning.

While sitting in the restaurant which is clean, bright, and large for a fast food place compared with those at home, you review notes of speakers you have heard and those you're still waiting for in the coming days. The conference has been excellent, as you expected. Interesting speakers, good material, A+ in all aspects. Not really much is new, however. SSDD. You remember when you were looking for postdoctoral positions and some of the institutions where you interviewed had "left the cutting edge in the dust." But those questions still remain entirely unanswered now a generation later, despite lots of good solid work. Much of neoplasia**, atherosclerosis, arrhythmia, fetal development and differentiation, degenerations, to name a few. And the scourges continue to re-invent themselves while what should have been annihilated microorganisms have found unwitting new hosts. Think syphilis, tuberculosis, polio.

The door you used to leave the hotel was on the east. For exercise after stuffing your face you walk around the block to enter the west exit. On that side is the main entrance and people are picketing the conference. There are about fifty, mostly young and white, casually dressed; the bulk are walking back and forth along the sidewalk. Some are carrying toy stuffed animals covered in red ink with parts missing; others shoulder signs, recycled props of a contiguous vigil, with tangential slogans like "Eat Me."

Others are standing or sitting in the shade, drinking bottled Water. You wonder if they have urinary catheters and made sure to take a giant shit before coming out today.

The protestors are antivivisectionists. Science, and the life sciences are no exception, does require experimental models. The sacrifice of animal life toward better understanding of human maladies is a regrettable fact, but necessary, you think. Any animal used in research should be treated in the most humane way possible, with suffering minimized if not expunged altogether. Anyone violating this is guilty of terror and promulgating horrors even if they are not discovered, tried and convicted in any state supported judicial system.

You walk into the hotel, using the circular door, and up the stairs to the mezzanine, to the main conference hall; you make it without too much trouble, recalling how you could easily bound up and down stairs two at a time when you were younger. Science is rarely political, you think, or at least it shouldn't be (although fiefdoms and cliques inside the ivory tower are as ubiquitous as any subset anywhere else in society). The Academy of Science to which you belong and which is the foundation of the conference has pamphlets available in the meeting hall, supporting the use of animals in biologic research. You glance at them as you walk by; you think about it, but don't take one.

After visiting some of the exhibits in the conference hall, you find a place to park and help yourself to one of the soft drinks. There are buckets of ice and caches of beverages throughout the convention center, this largesse being sponsored by one of the lucrative equipment manufacturers. You look around and assess the situation.

The hall is busting out with women. In contrast to the doll last night at the hotel front desk, most of these are butt ugly. You don't understand why a scientific or business mind requires a woman to relinquish her beauty. There are a few who are exquisite in every way, the kind for whom you would sell your mother to the Arabs; curiously, they are staffing a couple of the shadier booths.

The remainder, the bulk under the bell curve, are basic

adult females, some more attractive in some ways than others. How's that for being vague? Still all women have the essential and unique female components that warrant careful and assiduous inspection with a variety of techniques and instruments, in your opinion.

While all women are theoretically eligible for your further scrutiny, there are a couple subsets that don't make the cut, at least for you. Black women in general; you know it's all pink on the inside and as you have noted previously, you have nothing against black women in any fashion; you just wouldn't want to fuck one. It's you, not them.

You see a bunch of really dumpy women, approaching the body habitus of the typical scumbag PWT back home; these don't do anything for you either. Where do these women shop, you wonder? If you were their garment supplier, you'd charge by the square yard. This butt-fucker** named Cuz you inadvertently met at a university function back home surprisingly summed it up best. During your brief conversation he pointed to a corner where two women were standing and said that one was his wife. When you gingerly asked whether she was the one in the white dress or the flowered print, he responded, 'Pawkey, let me tell ya. I don't fuck no fat chicks.' And neither do you; accordingly, fat tubs of lard remain the only other exception to your enlightened perspective of womanhood.

You don't mind ugly and you don't mind stupid. With regard to the former, there's the classic triple bagger gag you think; moreover, you figure that there isn't a woman out there whose looks couldn't be greatly enhanced by having a dick in her mouth, preferably yours or pleasingly photographed, filmed or digitized if not. By pleasingly you mean well lighted, sharp images with appropriate close ups.

As far as stupid is concerned, what would you rather deal with? ALL other things being equal, a stupid woman or a stupid man? Some questions really are rhetorical.

All women by their very nature have some intrinsic value versus their male counterparts, with the above noted exceptions for you. Within those limitations, you have learned through extensive research, this was no avocation, that each has her own unique secret areas. After your first marriage hit the skids, you recall hearing otherwise from a young lady who was cutting your hair. You mentioned your separation without any other intent, trying to minimize your being a typical male where a woman was concerned. She talked about her husband and children. She went on to say that she believed most men find out pretty quickly that all women have the same basic equipment, thus becoming demystified.

You know that she was absolutely wrong. Just like their cheeks, eyes, hair, necks, noses, lips, nails, hands are distinctly different, you have ascertained that their private parts are just as individualistic. You can say with authority that women's breasts are quite diverse in terms of texture, feel, how they hang and bounce and separate; nipple size, color, texture and taste; symmetry; and naturally size and shape; there is also the question of how they fit on their chests. Similarly, their pussies and asses are unique. The whole presentation of their feminine triangle speaks to this but doesn't stop there. There are the obvious differences of pubic hair color, texture, type, density, and pattern of cultivation; then there are the various pelvic shapes, the prominence of her symphysis pubis, her waist. From there you can define vulvar shapes, whether her labia majora are small or not, her clitoris shape and size as well as its bonnet, the overall pinkness, and finally her aroma, flavor, and tightness. Lest anyone get the wrong idea, most (thankfully not all) of your back breaking investigation has been centered on secondary sources rather than on site analysis. While this type of research has its limitations, the evidence appears unimpeachable.

The data are also extensive and highly varied. So much so that just about anything one can imagine is out there sadly to say. Here is a multibillion dollar industry that has no subscribers; a marked contrast to the companies that have millions of customers, but make no money.

You shift in your chair, pretend to glance at the

materials you have collected from around the hall, have another swig, suppress what would otherwise have been a resounding belch, and continue your gaping. But in the process your mind remains drawn to these thoughts.

Depending on one's perv titer at any given time, he or she has available tens of thousands of sets guaranteed to cream their jeans. Women can be served up stripping or completely nude and everywhere in between, wearing variably bras, panties, thongs, garters, garter belts, stockings, bustiers, hats, socks, sneakers and obviously high heels; there are natural, groomed or bald beavers; there are infrequent bald heads, unshaven axillas and/or legs; breasts may or may not be cupped or squeezed and nipples may or may not be pinched, pulled, or pierced; speaking of pierced, there are additionally pierced navels and tongues of course as well as labia and clitoris rings and piercings; tattoos and tan lines may be featured; she may infrequently have her legs together but more often they are separated as are her vaginal lips, on her own or with assistance, sometimes slightly, usually expansively. Her vagina may be filled with a penis; dildo (of so many shapes, sizes, colors, and textures you didn't see how there could be such an assortment even with your liberal imagination); tongue; bottle (either top or bottom); speculum (there are many varieties depending on the view needed); non-medical tool with a phallic feature; vegetable such as cucumber, squash, carrot, sweet potato; fruit such as berries or banana; her fingers and hand up to but limited to her entire hand or someone else's digits and/or fist; with similar attention to her anus and rectum, at a separate time or simultaneous to her vaginal penetration, all with a perspective of her standing (front, back, profile, or angled), squatting, lying on her back or side, or on her hands and knees. She may be just past legal age or much, much older; she may be a beauty or she may not; she may be with one or more women and/or men. Naturally, just about everything that she can put in her vagina, can also be placed in her mouth, often while accommodating insertions elsewhere. Lastly there are the cum shots (real or synthetic), the irrefutable evidence of at least one participant's apparent pleasure, with semen being deposited on her pubic area, buttocks or anus, in her anus or vagina, on her chest or breasts, on her belly, and last but not least, and apparently many people's favorite, her face, mouth, tongue, nose, eyes, and hair; these occurring typically with further oral efforts on her part, after being compliant with regard to her other orifices; condoms are used sparingly but increasingly, thank goodness. The above is not an exhaustive compendium. You know that there is much more variety, but you figure that if the assortment above isn't enough to get one's rocks off, then he or she should probably just forget about it and go to bed; these folks would also fall into the category of the perv's perv.

Even women who are very pregnant can be found posing, typically being portrayed in a minimally more benign fashion than their non-pregnant counterparts, at least in terms of vaginal insertions. And you think, 'at some point at least, a woman must think, you want to put that where? And you want to squirt what inside of me?' And yet that is where babies come from. At least with the pregnant women as well as those unabashedly fucking, there is a completed or at least potential hole in one, that rarely being the truly desired outcome of the sex act however for either participant in this context or in most others for that matter.

After leaving the first adult film you and your college friend had ever seen, he remarked with sweat on his forehead, 'Gee Pawkey, sex isn't a spectator sport.' Obviously, phantom gazillions of other people disagree. They can't all be like you and the now retired district attorney who said on Friday afternoon evidentiary reviews, 'maybe it's porn, we'll have to look at it to find out.'

Your exploration had been strictly for academic purposes and you believe you have proved your premise; all women have some intrinsic value within the previously stated constraints. This was a former career of yours; another life; it was a good job but intellectually stultifying so you are now on plan C. You were never able to land one of the really great jobs after your insurance work like testing condoms (talk about putting in 110% of your best effort, never being late or leaving early, eschewing vacation time and always wanting to well, not exactly, hang around the office), designing feminine hygiene products, or being a gynecologist for a college of women. Nor were you presented with the devil's option at that time in your life. Like most horny younger men you would have found it difficult to turn down an opulent life having sex profess-sionally with thousands of often very beautiful women even if it meant possibly dying thirty plus years later from a horribly miserable illness.

After looking at thousands upon thousands of women so disposed, appropriately catalogued, you ultimately shift your attention to their faces, their expressions; yeah, their eyes and makeup are often additionally enticing. But it's their smile, the sparkle in their eyes, looking right at you, that has you wondering. What could these women possibly be thinking? You see no needle marks and they rarely have any significant bruises, but manifestly drugs and other means of intimidation and coercion can be relatively invisible to a mechanical lens. Some if not much available material could be voluntarily obtained and probably is, with appropriate remuneration, but at what price is a woman willing to humiliate herself in an ideal world and place her health at significant risk in one that is not?

Now you recognize that this opinion is at one extreme. The human body is a beauty to behold and human sexuality involves nothing that should engender shame between like minded individuals. And many women are rightfully very proud of their bodies. And you absolutely, positively believe in freedom of speech with regard to this issue. But these are someone's daughters! In this context the visual imagery becomes horrific. And they meld into the personification of the chattel to which women ultimately can be equated, since their original subjugation by men.

The answer to the earlier question regarding price goes to the concept of supply and demand, there being many avid sports fans with endless desires for entertainment, arm chair or recliner quarterbacks, rooting vehemently, usually with their dominant hands. These sports enthusiasts obviously have time to spare, being mostly from sexless marriages. You wonder also if they are simultaneously responsible for much of the existing graffiti.

You think about your marriage, seeing so many women sporting wedding bands. You learned quickly enough after your second marriage dematerialized why the dog became known as man's best friend. At least your dog sleeps in the same bed with you and she is always happy to play with you; not being a perv's perv you don't avail yourself of her devotion at the same time. You pray that your bitch wife is not typical, but fear that her numbers are strong and the evidence of adultery and broken marriages is telling. Just when you finally bought your second cow, the milk completely dried up. What a dunce! And so you figure that the average unhappily married male cannot possibly harbor greater antipathy towards his wife, unless he is on death row for having murdered the mother of his children. You allow that there are women who are in a similar fate, but have yet to meet one.

Nevertheless, your bitch wife has been relatively supportive with regard to other aspects of your relationship. She runs the errands and occasionally provides you mental comfort concerning the endless trivia of home ownership and pet maintenance. Hence, you decide to back down from a previously made promise and compromise, yet again, despite exhaustive resilience on your part for quite some time. You had told her you would never give her another thing. You reconsider this and decide you would like to bring her back something; the hotel has been such a dump so you decide to procure one of their really cool blue Water glasses. They honestly won't miss it (it's one of thousands and surely they plan for breakage), she will appreciate it, and the price is right!

You have finished your drink, your third, find an appropriate waste receptacle and deposit the container forthwith. How can people just set their shit down and expect someone else to clean up after them. These must be the same supercilious slobs who feel they are doing the "help" a service, their indolence and arrogance allowing for the latter's employ. Although you do draw the line at emptying the trash containers, mopping the floors, changing the filters, cleaning the bathrooms, cooking the snacks, changing your linens, and doing the laundry; you are paying for something, after all.

After making a deposit at the closest pisseria, you meander to one of the poster rooms; this session is devoted to nuclear receptors. You walk up and down the rows, making little more than casual glances at the titles. You're really watching the people. The number of FLFs** at this conference is astounding, both male and female. You imagine the corpulent, balding men with their jowls and stench as well as the still-visually-pleasing pumping away on some female and vice versa. Something that thankfully you will never see; while alleged amateurs were available during your academic research, they were of a certain aesthetic caliber if not well beyond.

Having watched people eat, your objective analysis posits what would people be like if they ate at home, secluded or with close, loved ones, and went to public forums where there are beds and other accouterments for having sex along with other couples (or groups! party of twelve, calling party of twelve!), variably engaged in satisfying their appetites for flesh. But then you think, maybe we should all piss and crap in public as well.

With your frontal lobes lobbing these thoughts back and forth across your corpus callosum, you head out of the conference hall. But not before finding a bag for some more soft drinks and the blue glass. The afternoon is gone. You trudge back to your room after getting some supper, an avocado salad with ranch dressing, from the hotel restaurant, which you take back to your room. Now exhausted, all you really want tonight is to be able to crawl inside a willing woman, some piece of ass. Now there is an expression that's always bewildered you; you really don't want her ass, you want her cunt.

And that reminds you of one of the other things that always bugged the shit out of you during your research into female heterogeneity; someone, somewhere, some lucky sonofabitch actually gets to enjoy the pleasure of those chicks' bodies on a regular basis. It's not a question of does she or does she not, it's the question of with whom.

By this time you have stripped yourself, plopped in the bed, and fallen quite asleep. You sleep better, this being your second night in this godforsaken shithole. How could the conference organizers have possibly arranged for the show to be here? Your dreams, like the night before are vague; you think some are from your childhood but you're not sure.

## Day 3

CONFERENCE FIRST THING in the morning. While there you see in the distance an old classmate; well, he isn't exactly old; rather he is a previous bud, where you did some postdoctoral training. You see him from behind and he turns at one point and you confirm it is him, but are never able to catch up to where he is standing. He looks pretty good from that distance. As you think about the uniqueness of people, you recall how you and your girlfriend in college, who later became your first wife, were able to recognize one another coming up and down the hill to the northern part of campus at a distance, just from the way the other walked. The fault that she ceased to be your first wife was yours, not hers.

Nothing terribly interesting at the conference; infrequent novel ideas scattered about; at least they all can speak English, the people, not the ideas. You ask a few questions. The answers aren't particularly erudite but it is nice to carry on a brief conversation, otherwise you'd wonder if you weren't going mute at times. There have been trips where you haven't spoken to a single soul for days other than when ordering food. You certainly can pay for that and other things without so much as a "fuck you too" to the cashier. On your dad's desk, he kept a pen set on which he had taped, on the base, facing his direction obviously, the cut out, typed salutation, “FUCK YOU.” While not necessarily the company motto, you believed this was a visual reminder when he had less desirables or cranky customers on the phone or in front of him. His view of the world: ‘as long as their money is green, they’re ok.’ That’s a lot more ecumenical than many.

Lunch, same as yesterday. While getting your burgers from down the street, to take back to your room, you pass by the antivivisectionists; they’re not only still at it, their numbers have grown. Law enforcement is putting up barricades. You definitely have your causes and reflect that it was fortuitous for theirs that they collectively had vacation time on the exact same days that your conference was in town. Nobody could do that professionally, although you suppose it would appeal to those liking a job with travel.

On your way back to the hotel you note a billboard for the mechanized greasy spoon that you just patronized. Walking past a store of overpriced electronic equipment of dubious origin, run by the English-as-a-second-language crowd, you recognize portions of a jingle for the same chain being blasted into the street. That’s carpet bombing the area you think. Well, they got your money--today.

You look around and take notice, identifying all the wares of the propagandists, pitched literally, in an effort to sway your thoughts one way or the other with regard to an issue or encourage you to part with some of your cash. There are naturally the completely unscrupulous who seek to separate you from your funds if you are lucky or usurp your very existence if you are not; while the former remain another story, you have considered this situation from which certain conclusions can be drawn; but again, you don’t wish your mind to go in that direction at this time.

With scientifically tested methods and statistically verified battle plans, advertisers wage their campaigns against you and each other. They enlist all media and some that you’d never imagine; with regard to the latter, the more outlandish, the better.

That being one of the first measures of efficacy; getting your attention. Whether from Earth's electronic lattice, bringing you programming as well as access to information from and contact to individuals and businesses all over the world or from printed media in all formats including but not limited to placards, posters, billboards, newspapers, magazines, and flyers, a message emanates, carefully concocted to emulsify your brain and bring you around to their persuasion or reinforce the obvious to the already faithful.

You see examples of all of these in the hotel lobby and bar as you walk past to the elevators where there are still more. As you go up to your room, you think, but at what cost is your attention wasted, their efforts like trying to mate a mule? Their costs are not important to you since they are parasites at best, superfluous opportunists, deluding themselves into thinking they play the part of ventriloquist for some, puppeteer to others; their involutional thinking is itself at some level a function of the current substrate amalgamated to the wafting vapors of their own poisons.

In your room you slip off your shoes and shirt and untuck your undershirt. You get the ice bucket and walk down the hall. By the ice machine there are more placards.

Walking back to your room, you try not to spill any of the ice which more than topped off the container before you could stop it. There is a message everywhere, you think, when you contact the world outside of your own mind and the opaque, hopefully sound proof and aroma proof crib that shields you from environmental exposure. Each an exhortation to do something, which may not have been on your mind at all. Which means that you are having to identify and process the message and far more often than not, discard it from your current or future plans to a sufficient degree that the only residual left is for comparing a repeat of the message which is sure to come and which can then be identified and discarded ever more expeditiously.

But regardless, when these moments are added up you

are wasting time. The written ads can be mentally discarded in fractions of seconds if your gaze should happen to stray their way at all. Those that are auditory or auditory and/or visual, become a ball and chain to your interest in the primary program they are "sponsoring," wasting a minimum of fifteen heart beats if not double or triple that, depending on one's baseline rate and the length of the call for action.

Back in your room, you fill a glass and pour some Water that is carbonated and sweet, but not fattening (of course). This ice is elliptical in shape, certainly more fun than the cubes you infrequently use at home; given a choice, you prefer your drinks not to require ice, since the melting Water eventually adulterates the taste. You sit in the chair, thinking about your options at this point. There is no one to talk to. You have no desire to watch anything on television, the programming is so limited. You don't feel like reading anything relevant to the conference or your work.

You pick up a novel that you brought, one that you had tried to start at home, but you can't concentrate. Your mind continues to return to your earlier thoughts. You put the book down, scoot down in the chair, allowing your head to rest against the back, close your eyes and start thinking again.

The subject matter of the propagandists is, unfortunately, or perhaps thankfully, relatively limited in scope. Think in terms of human desires and needs and the list races to redundancy; but the output diverges exponentially; perhaps this is the true and only perpetual motion machine.

Among your personal favorites, ranking high for irrelevancy, are the so called big ticket items or durable goods, which in your mind includes PCDs; these can be pigeonholed into the file of expensive necessities that you damn well better not have to purchase again for a substantial period of time.

And so you are inundated with typically unimaginative but finely honed proposals that offer to fix a problem you have or may encounter or allow you to fulfill an ongoing, basic need. Nevertheless, you have yet to purchase a motor vehicle, major appliance, or home improvement/repair that you wouldn't have anyway. When you decide it is time, you look over your options and then forge ahead. No amount of bravado, playing to your ego or baser instincts, is going to get you to do otherwise. And whenever you see an ad that starts with 'let's get right to the point,' what you hear is, 'this ad is costing me a fortune and I need the business, so get your ass in here.' An entreaty that is sure to make that establishment the last on your list with which to do business.

In the penny ante crowd, the product and its endorsement become even more ludicrous. New and improved "everything;" you're hardly the first to determine that this charade immediately invites the question that the old product was somehow inferior after all, which it is unquestionably by any objective measure. And your definition of new and improved hardly equates with business's.

To wit, you frankly don't want to hear about any "new" clothing detergent or machinery for example until models are available that work together, fetching the clothes through appropriate conveyances from the hamper, sorting them, washing and drying them, folding them and/or placing them on hangers. You are willing to send them back to your drawers and closet. And the chemicals required should be of quantity and quality sufficient to dispense you from having to dispense them more often than annually. [DJS: The use of dispense twice but with different meanings is one example of English's limitations.]

Same thing more or less for home and garden maintenance. One application should take care of the task, particularly cleaning, so that a seal is made impervious to the collection of subsequent dirt or grime, the ultra-thin protective coating, imperceptible by human senses, chemically thriving on the dust itself. Otherwise, you don't want to be bothered with the purported new advantages.

At this point, nature calls and you relieve yourself in

the bathroom of unwanted solid, liquid and gaseous materials. While washing your hands, you think about personal hygiene. In this department, the concept of convenience is basically the same but you wouldn't think so given the myriad pastes, powders, soaps, tools, potions and other chemicals touted to maintain or protect what you've already got, or rejuvenate what you've lost, and allow you to mix more freely among your peers, without drawing attention as an outlier**. You are somewhat more open minded with regard to these since they require application upon your very person, which requires a bit more circumspection and might, just might make you feel better.

You resume your previous seat, have another sip and again close your eyes. Now when it comes to food, that's another story entirely; commercial after commercial is aired, ad nauseum (literally). You are encouraged, no, entreated, to consume calories from the flesh of cattle (more palatable as beef), the bellies and muscles of pigs (aka pork), as well as similar parts of birds and fish and, depending on your domicile, sheep and goats as well as crustaceans, reptiles and amphibians; or their incipient young, before or after they would be able to breathe on their own, if not sequestered for someone else's sustenance; or their processed body fluids, which had heretofore been the nutrition for their young. Of course the propagandists, the experts at restating the obvious, those who can bring you something that is guaranteed not to rust, bust or collect dust and cures colds, moles, and sore assholes, they repackage this carnage into delicious nourishment that often times looks so good your mouth actually waters; now that's talent.

Nevertheless, these are the body parts, the cuts, promoted in affluent countries, the whole animal most probably being used in one fashion or another for human consumption in locales plagued with hunger and starvation. Not that the human non-consumables, the detritus of slaughter, are discarded locally; they are just used for feeding your pets or for some other use which doesn't warrant any further analysis one way or the other, merely falling under the aphorism, 'waste not, want not.'

Not that you want to think of it, but you can't help not doing so whenever these thoughts begin inculcating your brain. One man's pet is another's lunch, depending on the degree of the latter's hunger, the logical extension of which provides at least one answer to the earlier conundrum whereby one man's daughter becomes another's whore.

Offerings from the plant kingdom are also put forth of course, in the quest for a percentage of the food dollar; at least these don't require execution of a demonstrably frightened organism, struggling for survival, sentient enough to know its time is nearly up. Rather, nature's bounty of grains is offered without anguish and bloodshed.

There is just so much stuff out there; how much stuff does anyone really need? Yes, convenience is good and things that bring pleasure can become the lagniappes of life; but often they don't, going from an obligatory gift table or a fleeting "want" to the dusty tomb of the not-really-needed after all. Even you inadvertently collect so much stuff that you need stuff to house your stuff, at home if you're lucky, and at some other location if you're not; having to rent a facility to store your stuff should be a wake up call that you have too much shit and ought to do some major sorting and pitching.

With regard to clothing, the only questions should be, is it comfortable, will it provide the service that you are looking for in terms of protection from your environment? Rather than how does it augment your appearance? If the primary questions are an affirmative, then the only other concern becomes, do you at least not look badly in it? As far as quality which bespeaks to longevity of the item, how many garments have you actually worn out?

There are services, the sector that will do things for you that you need to have done but that you either can't or won't do for yourself or can't get someone else to do for free. These are espoused always to be cheaper and more accurate, which by definition then means that those who did business with them before were rubes.

There are the baubles which have been hoisted as the

tangible pennant of love and commitment as well as the not so subtle message of one's wealth and subsequent power; wearing expensive jewelry or its variations connotes one has money to throw out. It has long been known, a warning to others that if one so adorned has so much that he or she can afford to waste it on something so irrelevant, the owner would come after them or have someone else come after them with both barrels should they decide to fuck with him or her. The one exception to this category in terms of lack of necessity is gold itself, since gold is money, having a 5000 year history as such, much more a woman's best friend than any carbon fragments regardless of how the latter are arranged.

The penultimate consumer of the propagandist's attention is the entertainment industry. Here is a group less eclectic than the individuals would like to admit, their work being an integral in the calculus of life. For their very work product is part of the propaganda itself. In contradistinction to the amusement provided by a rare advertisement, part of the process of having defined salience and lassoing one's attention, the primary stated goal of those in Hollywood and all its divinations is to entertain, to wow you, to make you think and wonder and laugh. This is their stated goal; their real primary goal obviously is to line their own pockets at levels that the "little people" could not possibly fathom. As one radio host once said, somewhat apologetically, when confronted with his outrageous salary and the copious offshoots of income that he was able to parlay from the work of his motor mouth, "Hey, I've got expenses." And so he does; a wife (cha, ching!), private education for his children, million dollar condominiums in the City, chauffeured limousines, clothing that is certainly of quality and looks good on him, restaurants that obviate the need for reservations from the "little people," etc.

What is infuriating about "Hollywood" is the obvious hypocrisy. The examples are legion but you will dwell today only on your favorite in this regard; cigarettes are not "cool" in any fashion. While denigrating any person who has inadvertently become addicted to the powers of inhaling burning tobacco leaves and complaining that sitting in the same room is eventually equal to breathing from tanks filled with the exhaust from a diesel engine, those in Hollywood exploit the habit. They portray smoking teens and even adults as protagonists simultaneously burdened and enlightened, placing them on a plateau above the fray. Or the bad guy smokes, which is a tautologism. From your perspective, the only programming that should ever include smoking would be those with historical settings that require smoking for a flavor of realism.

You have another sip of your drink and glance out the window. You see people moving in the wing across the alley; their lights are on, but the shades are drawn. Shit. The Sun is beginning to set. You inadvertently glance at the newspaper left each morning outside your door. As usual, you didn't open it. What's the point? The names and dates are different, but the content is invariant and the ads will cause you to have projectile vomiting, particularly given the national election coming up.

So what of the ultimate propagandists, who are they? Surely that is obvious, given how society runs and the nature of Mankind. These are the politicians and their minions; while you grant that there are the obvious kooks and nuts who attempt to find a spot on the public's plate, those most successful align themselves into one of two main camps. Monikers and descriptions are so overused, the labels really lacking any utilitarianism at this point other than allowing one to know whether they should wear their shirts or blouses tucked in or not. While the general public and their representatives themselves would find fault with these definitions, from your perspective, conservative means wanting people to be independent of government and liberal does not. But these really shed little more than a penlight on the literal tip of the iceberg, the better part of the agenda being below the surface, never really seen.

In your mind the politicians are more alike than they are different but the latter does speak volumes; you listen to the aspirations and rhetoric from each camp and walk away thinking, yeah, you agree with those things, who wouldn't? What do you really want other than food, lodging, health, work for your body and mind, education for your children, a smattering of stuff, protection from your enemies both domestic and abroad, and a reasonable degree of diversion, which includes love?

But as usual the devil is in the details and further delineation of the above is open to millions of interpretations. Still, assuming that one can agree on what is reasonable in terms of the above, it is the implementation of achieving these goals for all citizens that becomes the burden and distinguishes one politician from his opponent.

There is the group that says, while all people are created equal, life is not necessarily fair, and so government must step in and take from those who can, giving to those who cannot; the other agrees with these two main premises, equality of life and the fundamental lack of fairness in life, but views cannot with will not, noting the obvious exceptions for those who genuinely "cannot."

Thus the debate really always boils down to two things. Are the floundering incapable genetically from surviving in the maritime of our society without some public Water wings or do they just not want to swim or, worse, are they waiting for a raft? And, of course, the bigger question with regard to needs is, what is reasonable?

With regard to the latter, there is no dearth of opinion in this regard. And while you see the criticism of such an oversimplification, this basic tenet begs the bigger questions.

Political debate similarly can be distilled to several basic tactics, which can be used individually or simultaneously, as needed. Never answer a question directly; always obfuscate the debate with tales of one's plans, actions and concerns; describe one's opponent's physical appearance and habits with flattery that borders on hyperbole because of the words chosen; and most importantly, always reinterpret the data allowing you to deny the veracity of the opponent's assertions, while countering that his group is guilty of the exact same failing!

The greatest sin, however, comes about when the propagandists join forces with the politicians, business, and Hollywood. Because it is at that point that the message, whatever that is, is directed with increasing redundancy. You quickly recognize that there is no great conspiracy at work here and make no assertion or pretense that there ever was or will be.

For with continuous servings of available goods and services and ideas, at every corner in every context, your mind begins to give in, your neurons and values are vortexed by the very repetition of the message. How many times do you have to hear about cars and boats, furniture and appliances and domiciles you will never buy, vacations you will never take, food you will never eat and stuff you will never buy before the obvious dawns upon you. Someone, somewhere is partaking of and enjoying these things.

Your very nature is pulverized and little cracks are instilled in the armor that your values provide your psyche. When confronted with relentless reveilles to shop and consume and eat and spend and experience and enjoy, who alive can completely resist? Thus the chasm between what you think you need and what you are told you should want over and over and over yet again becomes bridged by familiarity if nothing else. Hell, the propagandists surmise, you just might be more receptive next time, and at the very least, they have captured your attention. Walk into any market in this country and you can only conclude, if this isn't the land of plenty, then such a place will never exist on Earth. And the burden to consume in some countries is almost ineffable, it being difficult to hog far more than their fair share of Earth's resources.

With respect to the entertainment and other media available, much programming is allegedly free. This is an obvious falsehood to anyone who has ever paid a lattice bill, which includes communication devices and video and audio programming brought into their household. Certainly magazines and newspapers, choked with advertising, are not given away; so you wind up paying for the stories already subsidized by advertising revenues, while at the same time exposing yourself to Messages.

But putting the source of support of the media aside, what of the programming itself? The options are pitiful, you think. You consider the televised news, a pseudo-contrast to the rag on the desk you noted earlier when you got up to look out the window. You determined long ago, no rocket science here, that at any given moment there are a number of happenings occurring statistically throughout the world. It becomes a frightening prospect to think that somewhere, someone is being murdered, raped, molested, beaten, or ripped off in one manner or another. Women are being exploited, people are dying of old age and disease, babies are being conceived and born, people are falling in love and being married, war is being waged, tenderness and charity are being offered, problems are being solved, questions are being asked, accidents are occurring, children are learning, goods are being designed and produced and raw materials are being mined or grown. There are also records being broken, hope is being engendered, and animals are being slaughtered for food, or sport or worse.

So the real dilemma is, what of these events from the quagmire of civilization do you really want to know about when you want to know what is going on in the world? If you say only those that impact you or have that potential, the list becomes miniscule very quickly. Particularly if you define impact as something that affects you and for which you in turn can alter your plans accordingly. But the news services will discuss whatever they think their general audience would like to know about in a program and in a sequence that they think is best, always interrupted by the sponsors after no more than a few measly minutes' consideration. Multiple times during the airing itself, with the same message in the same format, with the same message in the same format, with the same message in the same format, with the same message in the same format, over and over and over until you aren't sure whether you should shit or go blind; you think, there oughta' be a law. So you hear about all the gut wrenching murders and accidents, war updates and other pandemonium whether you wish to or not. At least the news stories on the lattice can be selected by you as you wish to read them. But when you really get down to it, does it really matter one way or the other about most things if you give any kind of a shit or not? To you or anyone else?

The other programming isn't significantly better. There are the dramas, often centered around crime, almost always violent crime that includes murder in one fashion or another. The characters' personal lives function as the obvious foil on which to contrast the good versus evil saga being described. Practically any story can be portrayed by magnanimous sprinklings of the seven deadly sins and their obvious congeners, either daytime or primetime, the latter for all intents and purposes being neatly resolved in an hour's digress, another reminder that "bad" behavior doesn't pay. Some fortuitously portray growth and evolution not at the expense of wanton violence, but they are rare.

You wonder, how many bullet ridden bodies, mutilations, rapes, cons, car crashes, explosions, molestations, kidnappings, threats, terrors, and thefts can you reasonably observe, without becoming somewhat immune to the violence? There is a long standing voice that has objected to violence in the media as being a precursor of reality imitating art; given how the depravity of Mankind has conspicuously antedated modern media, you don't see this is as cause and effect, but it certainly doesn't help the situation. Just about everyone would have to agree.

Your criticism of these dramas really turns on the question of the veracity itself and the bigger question that it begs, which is why would anyone want to watch this stuff anyway? Everyone other than the criminals knows that crime is hardly a great vocation. Although depending on one's skills, or lack thereof, he or she could factor this into their retirement planning, the orange jump suit as the booby prize confirming their lack of adequate talent and preparation. Your life is unmistakably unique, but you don't typically encounter violent or other crime, excluding stupidity, on a regular or even sporadic basis, thus having no personal experience with which to contrast the fictional accounts or the actual breaking news that you are force fed. Thank goodness, most people you know don't either. So why would you want to hear and see these anecdotes? Anyone who actually has become a statistic either directly or through loved ones certainly wouldn't. You already know that crime makes for a limited career and you don't necessarily revel in the sedate nature of your existence on the basis of the misery of others.

In some dramas, there are accidents, twists of fate, that place life and limb in jeopardy. You already know the world is a dangerous place, particularly as people manipulate their environment, but again, seeing how others suffer doesn't necessarily make you feel good. Particularly when the amicable resolution of their predicament is a very safe bet indeed, within the limited time constraints to boot.

There is the weather channel which is for all intents and purposes worthless in terms of convenience. Unless your terrestrial coordinates unhappily happen to have been chosen in the dark lottery of environmental mayhem, being the storm du jour, your local weather won't be addressed in any detail, anytime soon, after turning your attention to that which you could easily determine for yourself by looking outside. At this point you stand by the window, look up at the sky and observe how people are dressed walking by at the end of the alley.

It is now all but dark, the city lights have long come on, and you are pacing in your room. You think you must be a sight in your shorts, undershirt, and socks, your pants having been ejected to the bed long ago. You finish your drink and open another. Hearing the relief of pressure and the fizz to come calm your tension. Placed in the ice bucket, these are already cold. You have a refreshing gulp; too much, too fast, some comes back up through your nose and you feel the hair on your head tighten.

Your thoughts continue as you lay on the bed now, with

just a light cover tucked over your shoulders. There are the programs that aren't scripted, depicting the contestants or players either in an actual game or in an environment that spans many episodes and observes how they respond to emotional or physical stress with their playmates, often with competitive stakes to add to the suspense. The former can be interesting and educational. The latter, get real, you think; anyone whose life is so sanguine that this shit becomes interesting needs to get off his or her ass, and go outside and actually undertake some personal experiences.

There are the jackasses, variably accompanied by representatives of the barnyard bedlam if the guests are not scumbags by design. You can't wait to hear their pithy ripostes. There are the comedies; simplistic setups, with characters who, like their Hollywood counterparts, almost never have to address the concept of limited funds in any way that you find credible; but putting that aside, their foibles and needs are exposed through sarcasm, cynicism, irony, buffoonery, and innuendo, occasionally with growth, and often at least with a few laughs being extracted from the audience.

There are the movies which, even with premium channels, have such repetition that you'd think since the inception of motion pictures, there have been only a couple thousand films ever made. They want to know why subscriptions are down. How about not showing the same film, three days a week, at least monthly or every other month? Yeah, you caught that one the last twelve times it was aired. Yeah, you remember what happens.

The shopping channels; just what you need, more stuff. The sports channels, great if one is into that. The religious channels, where the greatest prayer is for that collection box to overflow with the joy of the Lord. Music videos, increasingly produced and appreciated by those who have done way too much acid. The educational channels; generally excellent stuff, but with a bit too much repetition. Science fiction—either you're a devotee or you're not; too often trite, but occasionally brilliant. The infomercials, a shopping channel that can't even change the product;

that's not entertainment, that's purgatory. If you had to watch those, you might just as well dig a hole in the backyard and jump in. Children's programming: fine if you're a kid. Cartoons: fine if you're a kid or an unemployed chemistry dilettante with a home lab and a sexless marriage. The financial channels: a subset of the news, but with the personal reminder that no matter what you did with your investments, it was probably wrong, once again.

You sit up on the side of the bed for a moment and then go to the desk chair and turn on the light; before having a seat you get your soft drink from the nightstand, empty the glass and then refill it. Wait a minute, you think. You mentally return to the news and current events in general. There's a helluva lot of crime over and above the everyday publicly sanctioned workings of the government at all levels. Why is that, you wonder? Surely between the actual and scripted crime dramas, even the most saturnine numbskull would eventually learn what's what. Obviously neither of these individually or collectively is sufficient to dissuade many from pursuing this one way road to oblivion. You don't believe in predestination; thus that would then mean necessity at some level made him or her "do it." Referring back to everyone's basic needs, noted above, you wonder again, what is the problem? You know your taxes certainly are an emollient in the daily struggle of perdition. So if both sides of the aisle are committed to helping the cannots or will nots or whatever nots, then what they are providing would not appear to be enough or at least not in the right prescription. In other words, whatever the government is doing, it isn't working.

You put on your headphones and begin listening to your favorite love songs; you can listen to the same tune or even the same four second subset over and over, sometimes hundreds of times over a couple hours; one weekend when you took your son to visit friends across the state, you listened to the same three and one-half minute piece all weekend long. But the music now is just background to your thoughts, which are clearly lit and focused toward reaching a geocentric orbit.

And why are governmental designs falling short? There may not be enough money to go around; government could increase further the taxes on the already wealthy, maxing out with a 100% tax on income over a certain level. This would bring in a one time windfall. No high earner need ever work to a sufficient degree beyond his maximum salary and no company foreseeing the need to compensate their employees above that figure, at least not with taxable remuneration. So that won't work or isn't practical.

Besides, you know that seeding a field with money won't grow a money tree anyway. Which ultimately means again that government hasn't done its job right. And why is that? The answer to that question goes to the nature of politicians themselves. Whenever you hear a politician say that he just doesn't see how this program or that undertaking is going to pass the vote or be in the public's best interest, what you really hear is, "I haven't yet figured out a way for me or my close constituents or family to profit from these changes." Therein is at least part of the problem; everyone has their own agenda and the truly selfless individuals are chimeras in our society.

With respect to politicians, the plebeians want someone to govern who won't be tempted by the power and the sirens of corruption; which means that they are already wealthy; which means that they are either probably somewhat less than scrupulous already (no truly great fortune was ever made without the annihilation of some competitor in one fashion or another) or they are namby-pambies who were born to it, which would further mean that they have no grounding in reality. Does one actually think that faced with a policy decision that would financially strap a politician or his handlers, he is going to vote himself into the poor house? When was the last time a politician voted for a reduction in his wages or benefits? You know that with respect to the latter at least, certainly not the former, it has happened but you also know that it is absolutely not the way to bet. Either way, once spoiled, one has only the incentive to maintain and grow further the amplitude of their net worth, which requires thinking of Number 1.

Why else would everyone at all levels at all times be agreeable to additional gimmicks, over and above their daily routine, in an effort to harvest more green? Thus there are endorsements, children's books, art books, magazines, columns; singing if you are an actress or acting if you are a musician; there are goods and services that a celebrity designs, which is slightly different but a variation of endorsements. And there are the most egocentric of all, the autobiographies, which ask you to pay to learn more; rarely limited in their scope other than to portray the wunderkind's best profile and minimize the soiled doilies on their table. Finally, there are the charitable events, which bring the celebrity's name once again into the public forum.

Why else would so many of your average douche bags be looking for celebrity itself, doing whatever it takes short of crime to become "known," hoping to launch that brief notoriety to the stars in the firmament of public opinion? They see their role models, the athletes, musicians, thespians, rarely the commentators or politicians, always pushing the envelope, to be seen as more cool, more goofy, more outlandishly dressed, more beautiful, more risqué, more insouciant, more indefatigable, more pugnacious, more generous, more insightful, more stoned, just to be brought forth once again for public scrutiny that falls just short of outrage, which would make them an outlier; which would gut the golden goose. The distinction between contempt and worship is a fine one you think; perhaps this is a corollary to the divergence of madness from genius.

Thus financial incentive remains an overriding need for one to perform, to excel apparently. You can live with that, you think, turning on the television, despite the heat that will be thrown off. The room was hot when you came in this afternoon and it hasn't cooled down much despite being turned to maximum cold. Nevertheless, you are now bored out of your gourd. You rinse out your glass and go for round three: the bubbles delight your tongue and palate.

While you take your seat, rotate the screen toward your direction, adjust the lights and have another sip, you figure that you can handle a dose of the contemporary opiate, the tranquilizer that doesn't provide tranquility, but instead for most at least, stirs the pot and results in a paradoxical reaction, with stimulation instead. You learned long ago how to watch television and actually critique the talent. You do so without the sound; without this aural distraction or the visual obfuscation of subtitles, you can really observe eye blinks, raised eyebrows, mouth movements, and the whole gamut of facial expressions. You are no longer surprised by how ridiculous so many appear and how well a few do, when their acting isn't festooned by the shroud of voices and lines.

Muting the television also makes the manic disruptions of the propagandists much more palatable; ditto with observing the actual presentation of their messages.

Which brings you finally, and you are getting tired, the hour is quite late, to those messages once again, at least their content. There is still something wrong with this picture you think, cogitating further about the turd in the punchbowl. Billions of dollars are spent by businesses developing, refining, and then promoting very basic goods and services. Is the production of toothpaste, or an automobile or most any other doodad so onerous that competition is required to insure innovation? Can businesses not get together or be directed by government to quit wasting time on such mundane issues, pool their resources, craft the definitive product, and be ready for updates and other support as needed? Thus, allowing them to turn their full attention and efforts to other, obviously more important issues. Putting aside the question of monopoly, with mandated, generous, but not outrageous remuneration for said work, must they have the threat of some other upstart or established competitor goading their efforts? The answer to that is about as veiled as a nipple in a transparent bra you think; this has certainly been tried before and was a resounding disaster, just like the economies still in existence with state controlled planning. An individual pecuniary motivation thus appears requisite for progress or quality control, being the spur that prods the industrial horse to the finish line, while simultaneously and surreptitiously also playing the role of a different spur [DJS: ibid], this one under the fabric of society.

At this point your mind feels like a crispy critter. It is very late; you are yawning; you are deader than dead. You turn off the television, not having watched jack shit, and all the lights but the bathroom, put the white noise maker on, throw back the comforter so you don't start sweating while asleep, and root among the sheets. While trying to fall asleep, your thoughts return to the conference which begins anew first thing in the morning. Too bad, you think, that you can't attend somewhat later; maybe you'll skip the first hour and actually get something to eat, like a sweet roll or croissant or sticky bun. Damn, those sound good right now, salivation actually begins to wet your tongue. You could go out and get a snack. Maybe you should, you think; you're going to need more drinks after tomorrow morning's wake up rations. You'll worry about that tomorrow, you think, as you drift to sleep. Fewer dreams that you recall; in the morning you know you will feel more refreshed and be anxious for something to eat.

## Day 4

Your room still remains hotter than you would like; you wake up drenched in sweat. You speak with the bitch wife and determine finally why she hasn't been calling back. She was, in fact, but the calls just weren't ringing to your room. What a pain in the ass. This reminds you of the time in another hotel when you answered the phone and the woman calling was asking about the availability of a certain shoe! Despite explaining to her that she had reached a guest in a local hotel, she insisted that the phone number was correct and repeated your room phone number back exactly. Anyone who thinks the telecommunication industry doesn't fuck up is either on their payroll or has a really good dealer.

Now there's something, you think, as you begin sorting through the papers and handouts, articles and propaganda that you have been accumulating during the meeting, that requires no propagandists whatsoever for proliferation: drugs. Mind altering or numbing, as the case may be, chemicals; better life through chemistry your naughty frat buddies used to say.

What an industry. No obvious promotion other than the negative messages put forth by government, which spends huge amounts of GDP fighting the scourge; alcohol (yeah, that's just another chemical) is taxed and regulated, there being attempts to minimize underage use. No such luck with illicit drugs; they're ubiquitous. They are the preferred anesthetic for much of the young and certainly much of the adult world.

After discarding the conference detritus into the appropriate receptacle, you contemplate the task of packing. These thoughts are so mundane that your body goes on autopilot and your mind returns to the previous topic: getting high. That is a profession for some, typically but not always, scumbags of one color or another; addiction is certainly colorblind. It is an avocation for many celebrities as well, some having blurred the distinction between what they can and should be doing, perhaps by the powers of the drugs themselves. With considerable effort, they can sometimes root their way back to nirvana, without the drug's inspiration on which they had come to depend; sometimes they can't and their lives deflate, eventually forcing from their bodies not only the shit, but the shit-to-be. What a waste, you think. That's sad.

You personally have known people whose lives were ruined by illicit drugs and you have also seen others whose lives were ruined by prescription drugs, not by side effects, but by addiction.

Now here's some powerful shit, you think. Huge amounts of money; huge power over people's lives. Criminalizing it hasn't stamped out the problem; quite the contrary, some researchers believe that it has promoted violent crime as addicts do whatever is necessary to obtain their next fix. Certainly mega if not giga fortunes are accumulated by key players in this game; and it becomes harder to work for minimum wage when one's peers keep their own hours, making bankrolls each day, just selling drugs to their never ending clients. This is not to say that you think they should be decriminalized, taxed and regulated by the government; you agree that said legislation would undoubtedly promote their use at some level, even further than it already is. Accordingly, there would be an increase in the number of incorrigible addicts. But that number is hardly zero now; so the real question becomes, is the increase in addiction offset by the boon to government tax revenues, plus the reduction of government expenditures that would no longer be fighting the importation and distribution system, plus the attenuation of crime that must occur to finance drugs at the pauper's level? You grant that the other side of the equation would also have to include increased work loss and all the other expenses that accompany the delta that measures this increase in lives ruined, both for the individual and family and any others whose unfortunate paths they cross. You don't know the answer to this question and trust your elected representatives to do the right thing. You know they will, at least until or if the country completely runs out of money. At which point, other priorities may squirm their way to the forefront of the pack of necessities that only government can accomplish. You really have no idea; this is just a guess.

In the interim, with regard to the status quo, the supremacy of drugs is matched only by its two fraternal siblings; while they are not identical, familiarity with one allows a date with another. In the best case scenario, the anguished triplets of this unholy trinity all like to party together, but when times are tough, one will get you either or both of the other two. As any woman or wealthy person will attest.

Your packing is now complete, like driving home, a task done so often that you occasionally find yourself having gone by multiple land marks without realizing it. You reflect back to the conference, which this year has been outstanding. You have somehow managed to stuff the handouts and other paraphernalia, the blue glass and so forth back into your suitcase. It is tight, but if the glass breaks, no big deal given the price and the intended recipient; and you have wrapped it in such a way that it won't fuck up the rest of your stuff. You look around once more, making sure the place isn't a complete disaster and you haven't left anything important. In the bathroom, the towels are spread across the curtain pole, the sink is clean, nothing is on the floor or vanity that wasn't there when you checked in; the trashcan is full. All of the drawers are empty; there is nothing under the bed or behind the night stands. The closet doesn't have anything of yours left in it. And while you haven't straightened the room or made the bed, the covers are all replaced, appropriately layered and your personal trash is in the can. The door closes behind you and you check again the handle to make sure it is latched, but not before looking in your pocket and actually touching the key.

Downstairs you check out in the lobby. You look at the bill. What the fuck? Your daily connections to the lattice add up to six hundred dollars. Six hundred fucking dollars! And you were using a local access you thought. Well, it did connect just fine each and every time; but those same electron coated gremlins that change the clock by a half hour or so every now and then or cancel your screen saver, did it again. Your old access, which was used locally back home, somehow became the default again, meaning the fucking computer itself was able to dial out, along with a "1" and the area code, without any warning. This being over the telecommunications system that you didn't want to use to call the bitch wife because of the expense of direct dial. Six hundred fucking dollars! While there, you ask the hotel representative about comment cards for your stay, saying that, regrettably, this was the WORST hotel you have ever stayed in. She indicates that they are available, that there should have been one in the room itself. She then smiles and without further inquiry concerning your query, she says, “Thank you. And have a nice day.” You turn and walk away, wheeling your bloated suitcase behind you, without so much as a, “Yeah, fuck you too.”

# Book 3 Mother & Child

YOU LOOK OUT the window in the kitchen by the back door, setting down your book after marking the place. You put some music on, push your chair back from the table, and pull at the front of your blouse a few times for a little ventilation. Then you lay your head back and close your eyes, hands resting gently on your lap. You feel your soul is added to the instruments and voices that make up the compositions. After listening, truly listening for awhile, your neurons keep up with the tempo of each artist, singling them out in your mind as though they are the soloist, only accompanied by the others, first one guitar, then another, then the base, the percussion, and finally the female vocalist. Each piece can be mentally dissected, with pleasure in each group of measures as well as the whole work. You eventually look up, stopping the music as the clock chimes the hour.

Looking out again, you can see the Water, but can't hear it. You can also see birds in the feeder, others in the bath. The yard below is a plush bed of green, with trees forming various canopies and netting against the Sun's enthusiasm of this late morning.

"Are you getting hungry, Sum (pronounced more like put than putt and certainly not like poot)?" you call out, still enjoying the panorama of your back yard. You balance the increase in volume required against actually yelling across the house. Sum's room is across the living room that opens onto the kitchen and partially down the hall. At the end of that wing of the house there is your bedroom across from which is a guest room; opposite Sum's room is the playroom, where all toys are kept, his as well as yours and your husband's. There is a lot of noise coming from his room. No answer; your entreaty is drowned out.

You walk to his room, the racket growing ever louder; you know what he is up to. You're not worried; Prancer and Penny are on the job. "Honey?" you ask, standing to one side of the door and peaking in. No answer still. You see (and hear!) him banging on a drum with part of another toy; you're not initially sure which one. The other toys are playing music, too, including Penny the floppy eared bunny and Prancer the cocker spaniel. Penny is trying to hop around in time to the drum's cadence and Prancer is just running back and forth as though she has a rocket up her ass. At one end her tongue is forming a positive "q," dangling from her mouth; at the other, her asshole cover as you like to think of it (her tail had been docked a little short), is making horizontal movements but you couldn't really say it was wagging. Adding to the commotion is Penny's singing and Prancer's howling in response to Penny's singing. Even the lights are pulsating in a rhythm of counter beats to Sum's orchestration. You know he is getting hungry, given the time of day, but you don't want to interrupt him. You stand there, just watching and listening to the band known as SPP. He isn't using the drumsticks you noted as you first glanced in. What is that, you think? You conclude it is some of the girders from his building set that he coupled with his socks to make the striking end. Boom, boom, boom! He is really engaged, but it is lunch time. After that, you have reading time which he always loves. Still, you stand there, your left breast mashing against the wall next to the doorframe, your torso tilted and you just watch and listen, stretching out each millisecond, absorbed in the moment.

"Sum," you call as you begin to see a lull in the playtime; no answer. "Sum." You're being igged**. "Sum!" He finally looks up.

Grinning broadly, he turns and looks. "Hi, Mommy!" At this, Penny and Prancer sit down.

Knowing it is lunch time, Penny asks, "Sum, aren't you

hungry? Don't you want to go with Mommy for lunch?"

"Thank you, Penny," you say. "Come along, Sum; I really enjoyed your music and what you did with the lights; that was so clever! Can you put away your toys while I prepare the sandwiches or do you want some help?"

"OK, Mommy. I can do it myself." You walk out, but stand by the door, continuing to peer in. "Prancer? Penny? Other toys? Are you ready to go night-night?"

"We're ready if you are, Sum!" the chorus chimes with practiced synchrony. "Would you like us to go night-night?"

"Yes!" At that, the toys march, roll, walk, fly, or otherwise safely circumnavigate from the terrain of his room across to their respective designated place of storage in the playroom, all in less time than it takes for Sum to count to ten. Penny and Prancer stay in his room, having no interest in your lunch and not being requested to come with you. Everything, including Penny and Prancer, appears to power down, although (at least unbeknownst to Sum at his age), their sensors remain active. Penny lays down by the wall looking out from his door, toward the kitchen. Prancer jumps on the bed, lays down adjacent to the pillows, stretches out her back legs and tucks her nose between her front legs; she is also facing the door. Sum's room is now completely straight. The tiled floor is immaculate. The only other furnishings include a rocking chair, a cozy love seat, the small mattress placed in a frame that resembles a rocket nose cone aimed at the wall. The walls are decorated with soft pastels and there are artworks of many genres and themes, including a timeless scene with a boy and his puppy. Different seasons and landscapes, at varying magnifications and detail are also represented, some classic in origin, others made by your families over the generations; each represents contentment in some fashion. The lights at each corner of the room automatically dim as Sum walks out.

Seeing you, but without realizing your observation of his progress, he automatically reaches his little hand to yours, and clasps your pinkie. While heading to the kitchen, he asks, “What’s for lunch, Mommy? I’m starved!”

“What would you like?”

“A grilled cheese!!” he shouts, letting go of your finger and running forward to the back window to look out.

“Well guess what?” you gush. “That’s what we’re having! And then we can have our reading time. Let’s eat outside. The day is divine.” You see him intently observing, his back to you, variably shifting his weight from one leg to another. “Please take your hands out of your pockets,” which he does without verbal response but he otherwise makes no change in his position. “What are you looking at?”

“Nothing.”

“Well, tell me what you see.”

As you listen to him list the grass, trees, birds, the Water, you take the sandwiches, which you easily prepared, and the drinks and napkins. He marches behind you outside, to the table on the deck. As the back door opens, your nose is sprinkled with the salt in the Wind; from here you can hear the surf. The Sun reflects off the Water, their interlocking forming the adagio that plays to your ear. In the distance you see the pelicans in their V formations, some coming, others going, still others straining the environment for their nutritional requirements. You feel the Wind’s gentle embrace, your hair just barely moving; the long straight fibers on both sides of your shoulders and the short bangs over your forehead are black strands of such perfection that no animal would have the temerity to attempt a forgery and which are surpassed only by synthetic polymers. None of which Sum notices unsurprisingly.

“Oh boy!” he says. “No crust.”

“How did you get the lights to blink like that?” you ask, and take a bite.

“I didn’t,” he says, not realizing he has panned the question.

“Then who did?”

“Prancer.”

“Did you ask her to?”

"Yes."

"You're so smart."

"I know." The sandwich vanishes. He has something to drink, holding the cup with both hands. Like you, he is drinking Water that is carbonated and sweet, but not fattening (of course). He jumps down. Lunch never takes long when he is hungry. He starts to run around the deck.

"What about wiping your mouth?" You see a little piece of cheese on one lip.

"Oh yeah."

"With the napkin, please," as you see his arm moving up.

"OK." He then scampers from one corner to the other in the back by the door, rounding out to the semicircular other end, which overlooks the Water at the edge of the lawn. He is running his hand across the columns, thunk, thunk, thunk, thunk, making buzzing sounds as well with his mouth. He never stops; he just keeps going. You finish your lunch, witness to this unstoppable force.

"Go get the Book, honey, while I clean up the kitchen," you say, walking back in the house. The air inside is somewhat less moist, but otherwise just as pleasing.

"OK," you hear as his motion continues, now only walking.

When you go into the living room, he is sitting, carefully looking at pages that he can't yet read for himself. You sit down next to him. You turn and reach over to clutch him and set him in your lap. As you tilt your head down, your hair on that side, the fine black strands, brush against his head. As you kiss him, he wipes them away. "That tickles, Mommy." Just as you are ready to find your place with the bookmark, he says, "I've got to go potty."

"Good idea, Sum. Do you need any help?" you ask, knowing what he will say.

You sit back strongly on the sofa, stretching your back and then your arms above your head. At a height of six, two, you are tall, even for a woman; your husband is only five, six. You and your husband are so fortunate to have Sum, you think, refocusing your attention. You were married over twenty Rotations before he was conceived; he truly stands as a testimonial of your love. Children are one's greatest treasure, you think.

You met your husband through an ad, his actually, from a dating service. You had done lots of dating, certainly, and had many friends who remain very fond to you to this day, but you had not completely fallen in love. For a lark, you investigated one of the agencies, just to meet some new faces in your area, rather than having to relocate. You responded after reading it, feeling that it had been written for you. The message has remained indelible in your mind. He had compiled a short list of tunes, simply followed by: If these songs bring as much peace to your heart as they do mine, we should meet.

Sum comes running back in, somewhat unsteady on his little legs. Well, you think, that's why they call them toddlers.

As he assumes his previous position, docked to the mother ship, you find where you had left off yesterday. But before you can get out a single word, Sum can't control his excitement. "The story is very old, right, Mommy?"

"Very, very old," you say. "Ancient."

"Like my bed?"

"Yes, sweetie, like your bed. The nose cone of an 'ancient' rocket ship. You're so smart."

"I know." He pauses, putting his hand on your hand, which is resting on the book. With his other, his left, he reaches up and is not even aware that he is running his fingers through your hair.

You believe you can see the neurons reordering and new connections being grown by the look in his eyes and the automatic movement of his hands.

"What about Water, Mommy? And Wind? When is Wind going to come roaring in, Mommy? When are we going to get to the sex part?" he suddenly explodes, laughing and smiling, his hands coming forward and trying to clap.

You take a breath, snuggle the pea on the pod, find your bookmark, and begin reading again.

# Book 4 Minister I

AT THIS LATE hour, the Moon is still high above the horizon, aggressively pursuing the Sun in its sojourn across the sky, swatting the brilliance of the stars in its path with the light it can only borrow. The windows are open and Wind is gently crackling the blinds. You can hear avian arias alternating with recitatives from the frogs and crickets. A dog is barking at some distance, probably the neighbor's several homes away. Yours have been tucked in downstairs, past experience concluding that a snoring dog or one that jumps across the bed is not the most conducive to the spirit of the moment. You have a sip of Water; it is carbonated and sweet, but not fattening (of course).

Your bedroom window overlooks the river and across the river is the other side of the City. The falling Water in the fountain by the swimming pool tinkles your ears; bubbling comes from the fish tank behind you; the icemaker in the wet bar just refilled. You look forward to relaxing in the hot tub later tonight.

"I had meetings with several divisions," you say to your husband. "We worked on development, mostly. The new designs that we discussed yesterday look promising. Several projects are coming to fruition."

"That is certainly some good news," he replies. "I recall there had been many setbacks along the way."

You turn from the mirror above your dresser, looking at your husband who is already laying on the bed. He has folded the comforter down, both of you preferring the simple, softness of the sheets themselves to the regal, velvety expanse of the cover. You are also less likely to get tangled in sheets.

You stand at the mirror, disrobed as well, removing your turquoise earrings. As each hand is raised to your ear, you feel your breast on that side pulled slightly upward. You realize your husband is watching your every move and let the left one play peek-a-boo behind your arm. You run your hands through your hair in the back of your head, first one at a time and then with both; you rotate your torso and head to watch yourself in the mirror, to best orchestrate the show you are providing him. The countless fine red ringlets float down to your mid-back, their radiance all but defying gravity itself; Titian would have been inspired and challenged to reproduce the luster and intensity of these locks. Your creamy, pink complexion, would have been difficult to faithfully reproduce by Raphael or any master, regardless of his talent. You do have some blemishes, but not many and certainly none on your face. You have no wrinkles, lines or furrows. Your mouth, rarely turned down, is relatively small, befitting your quiet, confident nature. Still, when you talk, people listen. Your eyes portend the seriousness and kindness that powers your heart. Your willowy neck and graceful nose beg to be nuzzled by your husband.

"You are so sexy," he says, with a look in his eyes that only you have seen. Excited by this, you vacillate your profile from one angle to another, variably exposing at least a few red flares of your pubic tufts. The prominence of the top of your pelvis, exquisitely symmetric, contrasts the winsome narrowness of your waist. "I love the shape of your hips," he chants, a declaration that always gives you a tingle. While classically well defined, your frame is not in the least bit bony.

As you turn to face your husband and walk to the bed, you watch his gaze triangulate your coordinates. He starts with your eyes, dividing your form into multiple triangles themselves, some inverted, some not. Neither of you has documented a list of all possible combinations of three sided figures that can be seen in a woman's body, but you know there are many. You don't walk slowly, but there is no reason to rush either. You enjoy the pleasure of serving him these hors d'oeuvres.

Your husband has seen you like this over 30,000 times you instantly calculate.

He smiles as you reach the bed and extends his hand, whereby you lie down together on your sides facing one another. One arm he tucks under his head; the other he puts around your back, clutching you to him. You feel his hair against your chest and his pelvis against yours. You look into his eyes and rub your nose and cheeks against his; his breath becomes a draft for your spirit as you inhale his aroma.

His hand begins to move along your back, encouraging your muscles to relax from the day's events. The tips of his fingers at times, or his palm and fingers at others, variably rub, caress, massage, and knead your near perfect integument, running from the nape of your neck, down to your shoulder and mid back, your side and low back, and now to your buttocks, always with the gentlest stroke. Still clutching him, you rotate as needed to give him as much access to your body as can be achieved while still remaining on one side. He shifts a bit, too, in order to extend his tactile love to your legs and feet, your hands and arms.

As you roll onto your back, he glides along with you, his hand comes to your chest and his face close to yours. He sprinkles kisses on your neck, your sternum, your forehead, your cheeks, your eyes, and ultimately your lips. Your breath mixes with his and your eyes meet once again for just a moment; then they close and the kiss continues. His attention doesn't stop there, his right index finger gently outlining ever smaller circles over your left breast, with just the lightest touch possible.

As the kiss breaks off, he pulls away from you slightly and smiles. He honks your left breast as you giggle. The little orb, as he likes to call it, springs back to form between alternating caresses; with another kiss, his fingers read the Braille message silently telegraphed by your areola.

His gaze heads south, directed by the molten, red

setting sun that you know caught his attention when you were brushing your hair. Your valley lies beyond, extensively explored, but always harboring further adventure. When you had just been married and explored each other for the first times, your actions were childish compared with the pleasure that only familiarity can bring. Knowledge of the unique intimacy that you have shared for so many Rotations serves as an aphrodisiac to your play. Your loved one is pleased by pleasing you in ways that only he knows how. The muse at the top of your valley orchestrates the escapades that follow, with much getting and giving, but much more mutual satisfaction, multiple times. If there's one thing your husband has learned over the years, it is how to knock the mercury in your thermometer out of the park. The sheets are soaked, your red curls droop, you pant, you smile; you're lying in each other's arms.

The wall in front of you lights up. The DCD** comes on and you are at once face-to-face with your Chancellor, in the wall-size display. He is looking right at you. Not only are you completely naked and drenched in body fluids, your legs are not crossed or tucked under you; your husband's erection has not yet entirely resolved.

"Excuse me, please, Minister Esse (pronounced essay)," he starts, obviously quite shaken. "If I may have a moment of your time." Without waiting for an answer, he continues, "I am fully aware of the time and expected that it would not be opportune. I wouldn't bother you unless this was of the utmost importance. You're needed at an emergency meeting of the Chamber, which I have called."

"Of course," you say, getting up and slipping on a robe to sop up some of the extraneous wetness. You offer no apology for being so indisposed and he doesn't expect one; his bewilderment is not from coming in on the aftermath of your love for your husband. You lean over and give your husband a last, brief kiss. "I love you," you whisper. He gets up as well and puts on his robe seating himself on the love seat across the room. You ask for a light fan to be turned on and the lights brightened a little. "Chancellor, should we speak in private?"

"No, Minister, that won't be necessary; we will welcome your husband's expertise."

You and your husband have never been interrupted. You have been Earth's Minister for three terms now, and this has never happened before. What could possibly be the matter? Nothing has prepared you for this. Your perspicacity immediately assesses probabilities. Not realizing it, your face flushes as the most outlandish scenarios come to mind at the bottom of the list. Tincture of time having made most of those moot, no longer did new Ministers orchestrate mock chamber meetings and negotiations. You try to remember who exactly was the last minister who went through these charades, concluding after his or her term that such precautions were probably unnecessary. By example, all subsequent Ministers have followed these recommendations and you have been no exception; that was over 250 Rotations ago.

"Minister Esse," he begins again. "You know as well as anyone how many generations we of Earth have traveled the stars now. We have seen many cultures and learned many things from the other worlds, some gentle, some hostile, but all civilizations that didn't yet possess ISDs**. But now for the first time, an alien ship has landed on Earth!"

"As if! At this time of night, I don't think this is very funny. Gags are fine, at the right time. And if some upstart has planned this as a drill, I would like to have been informed of this first."

"This is neither a joke nor a drill, Minister. I already checked before contacting you."

Your yellow terry cloth robe falls open as your hands come to your face. So much for the hot tub.

# Book 5 Scientist II

THE CONFERENCE WAS some months ago. Back home it's SSDD. Your research at the University is going pretty well, but could be better. Home is abysmal. The bitch wife will never get it, you think. The blue glass did make it home in one piece. She was happy to get it; big fuckin' deal.

Every day is different, depending on how one defines different; currently the news is of legislation in Washington, sponsored by the antivivisectionists. The stock market just continues to rise to new highs, long ago having proven that trees can climb quite tall if given the right fertilizer. Times are booming; consumption is massive.

But every night is the same; you never go to bed at the same time with the bitch wife. Why bother? What's the point? She couldn't give a rat's ass about sleeping with you, meaning that there is no fucking going on. Once again, fucking is among the first to fall off the plate of marital bliss, as it has been in your case, being premonitory of many other structural problems that were only fancifully addressed in the premarital state. She watches television in the living room by herself every night; you sit in your office, which is where you are now, working with background entertainment. Sometimes you listen to music while you watch television with the sound off and work or read. You can both watch the same program, she in her room, you in yours. She will occasionally camp out in the other bedroom at night, "not wanting to disturb you." Yeah, but her snoring certainly does, even when you come to bed hours after she has.

She has long been asleep when you drag your donkey** to the bedroom tonight; the only reason why you even sleep in that bed is because it is the main bedroom. If she's there, fine; if not, that is fine, too. You're not about to move to the other bedroom on general principles. The bed is big enough that you can go for weeks without even touching each other. You remember falling asleep one night, many years ago, thinking that you couldn't imagine sleeping in the same bed with that woman and not making love. After you were married, however, you learned fast that this simply wasn't on her agenda of things to do. There was time for every tangent and diversion on Earth it seemed, but never enough time to screw, unless you were willing to wait up until 2 maybe 3 am, when she was finally "relaxed" enough to go to sleep. Yet she always appeared to enjoy it in the past. So what is the fucking problem? How can you believe anything that she says, given her obviously fallacious pillow talk? Even if it wasn't the best experience she ever had, your number one priority with any woman has been to get her off above all else, since by pleasing her, you are pleased yourself. Under these circumstances, your gentleness, and so forth, you ask yourself why she wouldn't find the time and inclination to satisfy your needs more often than quarterly if it was a good year. At this point, again, why bother? If this is marriage, you don't want any part. When you married her, you really thought the two of you were going to have the world by the tail. Why not just leave her? The timing isn't right. It will happen, when you are ready.

Arguments with the bitch wife are relatively few and far between, unless you are so frustrated that you can't deal with the status quo any longer. At that point, the vitriol bubbles out of the beaker and even the dogs hide from the bellicose rantings. You're not violent and neither is she, thank goodness, so nothing other than your psyche is actually damaged. You grew up with a mother who went berserk on a regular basis, a teaching example of "things you should never say to your child because once said, even an apology can't take them back." Perhaps it was this upbringing in part that resulted in your dysfunctional approach to life.

While you don't mince words with her, you do watch what you say. You are careful in every verbal or written communication, not only with her but also with everyone else. Only your thoughts themselves are truly uncensored. As you assess other people, first thoughts, no matter how hard you try to avoid them, are often such that civilization wouldn't be what it is today if you could read each other's minds, it is intuitively obvious. Even with the non-experts among us, you can never really know what someone else is thinking.

You lay down; but before you do, you have another sip of some Water, carbonated and sweet, but not fattening (of course). You finish the drink; it is all gone. Between the noise maker and the fan and the air conditioner, the room is quiet. The bitch wife's snoring isn't so bad tonight.

It is 3 am; though you are exhausted, you flip and flop and toss and turn. You resolved before not to look at the clock after you have gone to bed, since knowing only a few hours remain before morning is not conducive to settling down and sleeping.

Finally you do fall asleep. A preposterous construct when you think about it. You don't fall anywhere, at least your body doesn't. Although now that you think about it, since your mind does fall from consciousness, no longer being aware of what the body is doing or much outside stimuli, arguably a lower level, maybe the local PWTs are right after all when they say that they "fall out" to describe any alteration of cognitive function other than "falling asleep." While first blush would suggest how this logically came to be, it portends an entirely inaccurate transition. Your mind doesn't turn off; rather it turns on in ways that it can't while you are awake. Which naturally begs the occasional hypothesis that maybe for the mind to be able to do what it does when you're sleeping, being of such intensity, that in fact you actually "fall awake" or "wake down," as the case may be. Doubtful though amusing and imaginative. Finally, given the nature of the process, you don't actually fall anyway since that suggests a discrete event, either off or on, rather than the slipping that must occur as one system after another is gradually shut down or adjusted for the coming reduction in sensory input or work that will be required.

So what actually happens when you sleep? Perhaps there is a crescendo of systems that ultimately results in a threshold reached whereby a tidal wave of events is unleashed. You're dreaming at this point about sleep itself, this being one of those scenarios wherein you know this because the incidents are so outlandish that they could only occur in a dream.

The real answer to this, as with everything else in life except for a very few questions that only a very few people can address, is, who knows? Nobody. When you get down to it, all biologic behavior, regardless of complexity, is chemically based; no magic here per se. Just how or why two haplotypes with appropriate packaging can lead to another organism that, when properly maintained, is fully capable of generating another haplotype at some future date is astounding and entirely unknown. Even taking this as a given augurs little insight into the other questions that should ultimately be able to be answered in terms of the physics behind which a limited number of large and small molecules interact, albeit in an infinite number of possibilities; like alphabets, but incomprehensively more complex, the system constantly in flux, the building blocks themselves adjusting at the molecular level.

You dream the Earth becomes a multidimensional pinball machine wherein you are reduced to a bucket of uniquely assembled chemicals that interacts with all the other buckets as well as the game itself. Even the game board is a bit player in the larger picture. This all boils down to electrons, neutrons and protons and their ultimate basis. You haven't been down this road in a long time, you dream, reminding you of some similarly unique insight put forth by a guy in college who had been one time too many into the mushrooms...

At this point you come out of your first REM sleep

period; there is an arousal and you become drowsy, just below wakefulness. You aren't particularly restless and your breathing and heart rate are fine; the overall tension in your muscles increases; you go into deeper slow wave sleep. Deeper insofar as the brainwave patterns are slower, the multiple other changes are of no relevance since their purpose, function, origin, basis, indication, etc remains entirely unknown.

You quickly begin dreaming again and you dream that you don't remember the last time your dreams were so varied and pervasive during a night. A bumper sticker reads, "Unhappy parent of a juvenile delinquent." Another, "trailer bride." And there goes a rescue vehicle, "Advanced life support." You dream wondering who gets the tyros? Now you pass a bank, a first national bank, indeed, or some other such nonsense, like "first ___ church;" why doesn't the last bank to incorporate say that in their name so everyone knows it? What's the secret? If they can't be honest about their name, how can you really trust them with your money? And a pharmacy by the train station, aptly named, terminal drugs. Now there's a sick mofo, you dream. Onto the aphorisms, no balls, no bananas; a revolver trumps any straight flush; he who owns the gold, makes the rules...Woman: You know you're with someone relatively new, or at least very accommodating, when ...? Man: She asks, where would you like to start?

The images aren't clear initially; then you recognize them from childhood, which you did enjoy for a few years, certainly far longer than many billions of unfortunate souls who are born to the crime of poverty. There is your poodle, Georgie and there is your Dad. Georgie is barking inconsolably at him. Nothing will make her stop; ears are down or back as much as she can manage, tail is down, she is crouching, barking and growling, ready to spring back with practiced skill. What is the problem? It's just your Dad. She can smell him; she can hear him talk to her; he is standing in front of her. He is wearing a mask; the mask comes off, she stops barking and begins a fearful, cowering approach to him; the mask goes on, she starts up again, jet propelled backwards; this repeats over and over.

You see it again; same shit, different dog. This is your dog, Calabash, the basset hound. The dog has gone nuts; she stands or sits depending on her stamina, but won't otherwise budge, barking and barking and barking. You brought home a get-well gift card, 1 1/2 meter tall, consisting of a helium balloon with a face, below which are paper legs that hover above the ground. The card has to stay in the back of a closet to avoid the possibility that she could wander into a room with this in it; her barking is so vehement, it unnerves you.

Must be a dog thing, you dream. Since you first got your Labrador retriever, Dune, she has been one quirky dog; only lab you've ever known that didn't like Water. But God could that dog fetch? Talk about hard wired breeding; in the dream you see her running pall-mall into a host of bushes looking for the plastic duck. Like the other dogs you've owned, she is devoted and obsequious, at least to you, like a dog should be. Yet she is now barking at you; she's not lunging or showing her teeth, but your appearance clearly has her unglued. What is different; what is wrong? You smell the same and look the same other than you are wearing something you've never worn, a bright short sleeved shirt with a pattern different from anything she has ever seen; you speak with her and squat down, extending your arm, palm up; she calms down and comes over slowly; head and tail down, but wagging.

You have an arousal, but immediately continue in REM; now you're reading a book about medical quirks of fate, a collection of patients whose damaged brains from one disease or another rob them of a feature of their humanity. Little focal bits of brain cease to work properly and people can't see things on one side, but still try to compensate; or don't recognize stimulation on one side of their bodies, not wiping one side of their mouth; or cannot recognize that their hand is their own or a loved one's face. How interesting, you dream, with regard to the latter; despite hearing a familiar voice, the unfortunate patient will resolutely deny that one is who they say they are, even though they can accurately describe the face they see.

The television is on; the channels are flipping; the sound is off; three or four channels are alternately shown in this dream; there are monsters, hideous creatures; some appear menacing, others not; facial expressions aside, as well as body stance and the display of any appendages the anthropomorphic entity might possess, there are the obvious overriding similarities, the distortions, perversions, borrowings from other Species that are equally aggrandized and freakishly portrayed; each artist trying to outdo predecessors and provide the audience with their money's worth. You attempt to determine the story line, but each program stays on for only ten to fifteen seconds before switching to another. You're trying to see distinguishing features that help you analyze even the genre of the program.

This is now a nightmare, you dream, as it continues. You're in a club; you're listening to this gamine who's come to your table. It's hard to hear because of the loud music, but her words are nevertheless quite clear; she is complaining. She is smoking, one after another, to the filter; she doesn't care if you touch her, but you might as well be touching a manikin so you don't. Her head hurts; her back hurts; she is exhausted; her boyfriend wants her to have a baby; she's been taking acetaminophen all day; she says she wants to go back to your place.

You awaken, this is no arousal; you recycle some liquid waste; you're thirsty; it's not time to get up. You finished your drink earlier; the cup is empty. What the fuck! You fill the cup from the bathroom faucet and have a sip of Water; not bad you think; actually rather refreshing. You down the whole cup and have some more; nothing in it, you think, but the price is right. You lay back down and quickly fall asleep.

This Water is rapidly absorbed; molecules are distributed all over your body as they go from your alimentary system to your circulation and beyond. Some enter your brain, at the molecular level, ultimately being incorporated at the subcellular level. The brain is a master of feed back loops, overwhelmingly suppressive, if it is anything. The Water interacts with a membrane channel protein, changing the shape, and ions begin pouring inside the neuron while others seep out. As this happens an electrical charge begins to develop moving down the axonal membrane. At the end this charge releases tiny packages of smaller molecules into the synaptic space between neurons and other cells, which then cause other neurons to fire, and still others, in a divergent pattern, at once removing some of the inhibitory circuitry, finite, but barely measurable compared with the overall apparatus. Still, a change is made as multiple dendritic and axonal connections are reshuffled and others appear anew.

You wake up. You actually feel rested. After recycling, more liquid waste, you hurry downstairs for something to drink, Water that is carbonated and sweet, but not fattening (of course). Those were some weird fucking dreams. You have an idea.

# Book 6 History

WHEN WIND CAUGHT up with Water, she was tobogganing down an obstacle course of falls, caverns, and rivulets. He had recently sprinkled her back to Earth as snow, the final cookies in their northern bakery class, each uniquely shaped by his gentle caress. There were no bad storms here. He felt good; no, he felt better than good. Not because of his labors of love with Water though he was proud of his craftsmanship. He was inspired when playing with Water, particularly when she was stable enough in his environment to allow his assessment of her in minute detail; thus his penchant for snowflakes. But that wasn't why he felt euphoria or rather smugness.

Wind felt smug because he was calling Water without any response. He was being igged and he knew why or at least he thought so. Water had collected her portion from the mountain range and moved toward the coast over the northern continent in the western hemisphere; she was now a singular, but massive river following a serpentine path through the desert. He finally got her attention with a massive sandstorm that threatened to block off part of the river from sedimenting debris.

"Yes, what it is, lover?" Water bubbled. "You've certainly got my attention now."

"What is the matter?" he countered. "Why were you ignoring me?" But before she could begin an explanation, Wind blew on, "Oh, but I know why." He delivered this challenge in a drilling and taunting cadence, jumping back and forth over her banks.

"I wasn't ignoring you, Wind," Water responded. She

was ignoring his unreasonable jack hammering on her shores, there being no overall improvement or significant deleterious sculpturing of her interface with Earth. "I was in deep meditation."

"Over what?" he tapped. "I'll bet I know."

"We already have an outstanding bet."

"Which is precisely my point," he said. "You are preoccupied over the fact that I appear to be winning by a landslide, no pun intended." He had calmed down considerably, the air now being filled with only small straws of movement. From the river to the horizon, sand and non-fixed desert detritus could be seen floating back to Earth, with little further horizontal motion.

"As if, jackass," Water hummed through the whirlpools, created by Earth for her at this juncture in their bed. "You just think you are."

"What kind of mood altering chemicals polluted you in those mountains? You can't possibly be serious. Let's check in on Mankind's scorecard," said Wind. He was picking up speed again, as the straws gave way to hoses of blowing air, pelting the underlying Earth and causing dimples in Water's surface. "The desert here makes me think of another time, rather long ago compared with the life spans of men, but not all that long ago after all:"

> It hasn't been a good day, you think. But with God on your side, you hope it will get better. It has been years since you have been home; you and your associates are starving; there is no food; there is less Water, the enemy having poisoned all the nearby wells; your situation is getting desperate; it is mid-summer, 1099. You are on a holy mission to free Jerusalem from the heathen now in possession; your faithful have been prevented from making pilgrimage. The Muslims are taunting you from the walls; they are cursing and flaunting precious treasures. You are angry, frustrated, bitter; you hate.
>
> Earlier on the trip south from Europe, you took

the opportunity to annihilate as many Jews as possible. Now that's doing a good job for the cause, you think. This great accomplishment reminds you of your faith and commitment to your duty and you become more hopeful that you will see justice done in Jerusalem.

At the urging of a psychic, you walk around the perimeter of Jerusalem barefoot; the rapture in your heart soothes the martyred flesh. Good news follows. Logistics arrive with sustenance and building materials for siege towers.

Jerusalem falls to you. You celebrate your victory with joyous praise and continue the slaughter. You and your comrades proceed to exterminate one by one each and every inhabitant of the city with the exception of a handful, who are expelled. You cut off heads, arms, hands, feet, legs; you disembowel; you smash heads with your clubs; you smash limbs; you break backs; you cut off ears and cut out tongues; you shred bodies with arrows; you gouge out eyes; you cut out hearts; you trample some; you set others on fire; you rape the women then beat them to death, strangle them, cut off their heads, torture them further, mutilate their bodies; every child is laid low. There are piles of body parts that are assembled; you and the horses wade through streams of blood; the city's Jews are herded into one building and it is set on fire. In the end, after two days, some 30,000 to 40,000 previous citizens of Jerusalem are gone; that's twelve people a minute or one every five seconds. The city and all of its booty are yours. A defining moment in human relations has occurred.

* * * * * * * * * *

IT HASN'T BEEN a good day, you think. But with God on your side, you hope it will get better. Your city has been under siege now for some time by the infidel and his associates; you have seen them starving and dying of thirst; you poisoned all the nearby wells; they have nothing further with which to attack you. Your situation is manage-able; you can hold out; it is mid-summer, 1099. You are the rightful possessors of Jerusalem and will prevent any infidel from making pilgrimage. You taunt your enemy from the walls; you curse at them and flaunt your precious treasures. You are angry, frustrated, bitter; you hate.

You see the infidel walking around the perimeter of Jerusalem barefoot; what an absurd ritual, you think. Bad news follows. Enemy logistics arrive with sustenance and building materials for siege towers.

Jerusalem falls. You and your comrades, wives, children of all ages, mothers, fathers, sisters, brothers, grandparents and all other relations are systematically slaughtered; there is no mercy; the infidel is relentless in his quest for revenge. The anguish, the misery, the horror cannot be described by any mere words on a page as you ponder your existence and imminent death as well as the ultimate safekeeping or demise of your loved ones as you watch others bent over and beheaded. Their severed heads kicked by the infidel into a growing pile, your own fate is perhaps preceded by the removal of your arms, hands, feet, legs which you won't need anymore anyway; you are disemboweled; your head is smashed with a club; your limbs are smashed; your back is broken; your ears are cut off and your tongue is cut out; your body is pierced by arrows; your eyes are gouged out; your heart is cut out; you are trampled; you are set on fire; your wife and other female relations, regardless of age are raped then beaten to death, strangled, their heads cut off, they are tortured further and their bodies are mutilated; all of your children are laid low, their bodies sport to the same

> defiling that ends your life. Your body parts are assembled in piles with other heads, feet, hands; the enemy and his horses wade through streams of your blood; the city's Jews are herded into one building and it is set on fire. In the end, after two days, you and some 30,000 to 40,000 previous citizens of Jerusalem are gone; that's twelve people a minute or one every five seconds. The city and all of its booty are no longer yours. A defining moment in human relations has occurred.

"Yeah, Jerusalem was a fucking disaster," said Water forlornly. "And you know I'm not one to use the F word."

"No shit," said Wind. "But that was a long time ago, right?"

"Right," said Water, but she knew better and she also knew that she had just taken the bait. This was her plan since he had disrupted her meditation. She had set Wind up for one of his desert typhoons, during which he would be relentless in arguing his case, whether she wished to listen or not, sand grinding against sand. There is nothing that you can tell me that I don't already know, she thought. But she was curious as to where his logic would take him on this tirade, how glib he would become, and how low he would descend. They hadn't repeated this argument in over 500 Rotations and she could use the stimulation, she thought, which was why she was conversing with him at all.

"Wrong," said Wind. "Fast forward to the not so distant past, to Jedwabne, Poland and one of that infamous city's residents."

> Any survivor knows what happened July, 1941; the situation was complicated and you knew nobody who wasn't there would believe you or understand. The problem had already been solved in terms of blame by the Communists after the war; tensions were already high; the area had been under Soviet rule for some time and now the Nazis were in the area. Some of the Jews were believed to be working

for the Soviets as spies; you heard neighbors saying so down at one of the stores. Your church was diametrically opposed to their faith; nevertheless, you had lived peacefully with them, though their synagogue was burned down about two years ago. Then the Germans came, just a handful; they brought film making equipment, both stills and motion pictures. Their work product didn't survive fortunately, but you can't get the slaughter out of your head. Many hundreds, some say well over a thousand, others say the number of Jews was equal to the number of Catholics in Jedwabne, perhaps 1500. You're not really sure the exact number and whether it was one or one million makes no difference since all of the Jews were slaughtered. After standing in the sun without Water for hours, then being clubbed to death, mutilated and left to die, games were played with severed body parts; some were shot, pregnant women were gutted, tearing the fetus from their wombs, children and babies were heaped upon the burning flames that hid much of the horror, only a small number of graves for bodies were actually dug. The remainder still were herded into a barn which was then set on Fire. Some of the Jews hopefully got away from town before the Germans arrived; the rest were completely wiped out. For at the end of that day Jedwabne had no more Jews; that was indisputable. Who is responsible for these atrocities you know; the horror tattooed the images in your mind forever along with screams and tears. These were your neighbors; under what circumstances could you be persuaded to actually perform these horrendous murders? The German agenda was spelled out to your mayor, with the encouragement to riot by some who are always lurking in the sewers. Germans hated Catholics, but they hated Jews worse. Even if it wasn't you but the Germans who committed these hideous crimes, you are still guilty

> through complicity. You know that was your only option since opposing them would have meant certain death for you and your loved ones. Your never ending nightmares and scarred memories serve as your punishment either way, God forgive you, for not having martyred yourself in trying to save another human being.

"And these are but just two meager examples," Wind unhappily boasted, quickly going on with the admonition that he didn't wish to single out any particular nationality, religion** or other distinguishing feature in the near infinite saga of man's inhumanity to others like himself. "Recall Roman ferocity that completely slaughtered entire villages that resisted a siege, reducing the population and even many of the animals to piles of body parts and these were surpassed by the Mongols. The list is almost not to be believed in terms of the number of wars and we don't even want to consider the possibility of his cruelty to animals."

"We've been there on this one," Water said. "Mankind has to eat."

"Of course, I don't begrudge him nutrition from any source really and you know full well that we're not talking about the butcher."

"Yes, I agree unfortunately with that issue; Mankind is a veritable bastard with regard to other living creatures, but I still think I will ultimately win our wager."

"Sure you will," his sarcasm clear and biting. "Such optimism in the face of the facts is valiant. There are ongoing and many thousands of wars that Mankind has waged. Think about what this really means. Society is willing to send young members of their culture, those who have everything in the world to look forward to and always someone's son, father, brother and so forth, away from their homes in order to kill similar members of their opposition and then become the law and order of that land, forcing their will upon the vanquished, or vice versa of course. The reason has to be simple and yet all powerful to command commitment of such precious resources, verily the future of that Society. Essentially, if the stakes warrant putting a grubstake of your future on the line, it must only be that the future itself is at stake. At least it would appear so with the organ grinding of the people's minds by the propagandists in their finest symphonic presentations; but in fact the real motives, pulling the propagandists very strings, are the ancient zombies embodied by the seven deadly sins. Thus war is justified, in all parts of the world, at any given time, just like on the more individual level, someone is being tortured or abused at any given time."

He paused after what he thought was a percussive finale. Water thought, but didn't say, I can see I'm not going to be disappointed today.

Misinterpreting her silence, Wind began again. "Do you recall the night Pawkey walked back to his dorm from his girlfriend's apartment in the middle of the night, very late? Her apartment was a good trek from the main campus, across the railroad tracks and beyond the factory parking lot. He had to go up the hill, past a number of other dorms; there was a full Moon; it had snowed a few days earlier and the Earth was still steeped in her white comforter."

"Yeah, I remember. What about it?"

"Well, Pawkey had been into some of the chemical refreshments supplied by a roommate's boyfriend. You remember him; he had the business cards with a rubber stamped inane logo about strange people and strange things. On the way home, Pawkey kept looking around, paranoid that monsters were hidden among the shadows. Of course, the kind he was thinking about, creatures and whatnot, don't really exist. But monsters do live on Earth; we both know that."

"Unfortunately, I can't dispute that. The world has spawned monsters galore."

Without acknowledging Water's lament one way or the other, Wind continued and was ever so slowly building up a head of steam. "In fact, I'll bet you somewhere right now a dog is being hung. How many times have we seen this horror? The monster with or without an assistant approaches the dog, the prey already wary that something is amiss; the dog can initially be immobilized or stunned with a club before the hanging or depending on the level of sport desired, it can be cornered and eventually lassoed with a rope or other high tensile strength cord with a nonserrating surface; all this time the dog is getting more and more worked up and panicky, with much growling, barking and showing of teeth; the ears are back and the dog will do some lunging; the rope is then thrown over a tree limb or other strong but not particularly high fixed beam and then pulled fairly rapidly so that the dog's hind feet are lifted off the ground; the point is to be quick enough about it so that the neck is quickly stretched and its air supply cut off, but not so quick as to break the neck. Then the fun really begins, as the monster watches the fruits of his efforts; the dog's size has all but doubled long before this stage as its tail has bushed out and its hair in general is standing up; the only vocalizations now are squeals and whimpering; the terrific salivation is reduced and it paws at the air, its eyes bulge, its tongue hangs out; it defecates, its bladder empties. It dies, leaving a lifeless carcass where once a vibrant organism had been.

"Or a cat is disemboweled or beheaded. For the former the monster has to be able to grab it by the back of the neck, hold on tight and work fast with his other hand or have an assistant do the fun part, cutting out the cat's guts with a long quick slash, straight or curved; then he just drops it and watches it suffer for awhile before it dies. For the latter a guillotine type apparatus works best unless the monster is particularly adept with a knife or hatchet, but there is the occasional monster who will break the cats neck first, then decapitate the poor thing. Animals can be tortured undoubtedly any number of ways, the most typical being by kicking, beating, or starving them. Even not giving them proper care is inhumane by definition, the perfidy of which can easily be extended without difficulty. Less than twelve generations ago, no literature was put forth on animals' rights.

"And as sure as animals are abused and hunted for sport, somewhere no doubt, at this very moment some man is being hung, for whatever ostensible reason. We know the real reason; think about the misery of the dog; then think about a human being; same basic scenario; the man is cornered, immobilized, his hands are tied and his neck is stretched, sweat blasting out of his pores and tears gushing as he screams and begs and he sees his life passing before him. As he chokes, his heart rate triples, his blood pressure pops a cork, all in response to the glandular explosion of fight or flight hormones, neither of which will get him out of this dilemma; he pisses and craps, kicks at the air, maybe even has a seizure if the executioners are lucky, and then he dies. Now that's having a good time!"

"Why are you telling me all these horrible things?" Water interjected over some rapids.

Wind just went on. "There are the general beatings, promulgated by a certain type of monster, not in the context of religious zeal or politically motivated. No, these are more selfish, a result of one's employment or as entertainment. At the very least, these beatings are a type of torture, meant to intimidate and set an example, or for shear diversion; for the same reason that a dog licks her ass, because she can," he gusted, now answering her last query.

His volume increased in amplitude and frequency. "There is the monster rapist, defined for this purpose as a stranger who forces himself upon a woman, for his selfish hedonistic pleasure, knowing in advance the horror that he will have indelibly etched in her memory forever, leaving her eternally violated in a way that no man could ever know or really understand unless he had been forcibly buttfucked and even that's not exactly the same. This monster may or may not beat her, cut her, choke her, burn her or kill her among many options available.

"Below the rapist is the monster that beats his wife or girlfriend and then expects her to come to bed where she can bounce on his dick, get on her hands and knees or otherwise bend over and take it from behind, or maybe he'll just get between her legs for a quick fuck or maybe he'll just get her to suck his dick, depending on his mood.

Maybe he'll have a serving of each since the beating always makes him feel more of a man and he can feel the semen filling up his balls and isn't that her job after all, to be the sponge for his ejaculation. Some days he can cum on her face, in her mouth, cunt or ass four or five times per day if she is lucky, and he certainly expects her to tell him how much she enjoyed it. If she doesn't express her appreciation and rapture at his touch, she won't be remiss more than once; the beating after that will leave her unable (even for him) to fuck for three days. As if the beating isn't enough, after that hiatus she won't be sure she'll ever be able to shower, wash, bathe, gargle, brush, douche or enema away the torrent of sperm that will come her way when he is able to start dicking her again. So imagine the terror experienced by such a woman on a daily basis, the dread when she hears him come in the door, this being the man that she thought she loved at one time. Actually she did love him and she certainly thought he loved her. Of course he will continually castigate her verbally and demean her; occasionally, when he is drunk and has a friend over, he'll actually tell him how she serviced him last night, in great detail, orifice by orifice, including where he ultimately dropped his load, both times, with them laughing and whooping it up."

Water maintained her silence. He's just getting started, she thought.

On cue, Wind wondered further, "Maybe in time her husband can share their videos with friends and maybe even have his wife perform with friends. What to do with these monsters?"

"You tell me," Water gently responded. At this point in the river she was serenely flowing west, with few areas of turbulence being created. Despite his progressive gyrations, Wind was nowhere near affecting her at this point in the afternoon.

"Maybe we should castrate them before hanging them. We could just castrate them and cut off their hands or arms but I would be concerned that with prosthetics, they could still be of danger to women; that's why I'd hang 'em. But only after cutting off their nuts. What do you think?"

"Gets my vote," she rippled, cleansing some stones.

"The ultimate monster is the child molester, of course, and we won't even go there in terms of the options and possibilities other than to include sexual, physical, and mental abuse. Suffice it to note that even compared with the level of terror experienced by any woman being beaten and abused, one cannot likely imagine the horror that would shatter the spirit of a child by the heinous acts and crimes that can be inflicted on another human being. These monsters are the absolutely lowest on the dung heap of scumbags to which Mankind can descend, even below the war mongers, murderers, torturers, rapists. May they be damned to be daily sodomized by the Devil himself for all eternity; and for good measure may the Devil force these SHPOSs** to stretch their dicks up to their mouths, make them blow themselves until their mouths and jaws hurt; periodically slapping themselves around the face with their dicks, only to hose their faces with a cylindrical jet of semen that fills their throats causing choking and gagging, sticking to their hair, eyes, ears, noses, that continues to ooze from these areas in a gradually decaying manner such that it's just about gone by the next day and time for round N + 1 of Hellish retribution."

And Wind puffed on, "These are the evil ones, that require intervention by government, falling into the category of diversions, now unreasonable. Why is man so intent on making some of his fellows so miserable; why is there joy in revenge and how can one be so indifferent as to force his will on someone that he doesn't even know, the most extreme of which is torture?" The last question was whispered to her.

At this point in her sojourn, Water lay placidly in a lake. She was sunbathing and didn't feel like responding.

Her stance caused Wind to begin his grumbling again. "People are tortured for political reasons, often but not exclusively to obtain information. These facts beg the question concerning how someone can be persuaded to torture another, assuming for just a fraction of a second that they aren't a sadist au natural; what kind of animal or monster, sadist or otherwise could do these things, at best oblivious to the screams and fear and pain and sweat and distress that their very actions bring on and at worst relishing in them? Surely the answer to this is easy; by reputation or by direct observation of whoever is in charge, the torturer knows that when the boss says cut off that man's fingers, all ten, he means business and if he isn't willing to follow orders, the boss will find someone who will. Moreover, just to remind everyone in the community of the implications of denying the boss's instructions, he will get the new boy to start on the newly unemployed torturer and his loved ones.

"Such is the result of absolute power at multiple levels of society, in all societies. At what point did intersocial relations allow one person to hold enough of a majority that he could command absolute rule, this being an adequate enough definition for the moment? Has there ever been a time on Earth when one group of men wasn't plotting the extermination of another, in one fashion or another, beyond the random murder or group murder of a family depending on one's need to be rid of them?"

Water jumped in. "Yes, there are a few subsets of humanity if the people are homogeneous enough. They have been known to exist, but I admit that they are miniscule compared to the general disarray of Mankind in his playground."

"Exactly. Thank you Water, for proving my point," Wind interrupted. "In fact, let's look at how this sordid creature, our progeny no less, came to be. Perhaps we can get some answers to some of these questions if we look at origins and evolution.

"A number of changes occurred that distinguished Mankind's earliest precursors. From my perspective, some of the most important changes included the eventual inability of a human infant to cling to its mother as she foraged with others. This forced mothers to stay at home, a base camp, and her whole physical structure changed as well; her pelvis had to enlarge to accommodate the larger heads of her young and she at some point became able to conceive at any time, losing the estrus cycle that marks every other mammal. Then again, at some point, Mankind realized the need to avoid incest; in these earliest societies, a woman became the ultimate bartering chip with other clans, perhaps this being the high point in the male to female relations game. During these times, collaboration and communication were needed as the men hunted larger game and the women stayed close to home raising the children. As tribes or clans overlapped there could be raiding parties wherein men as well as women would be murdered but Mankind was not yet waging war. Still, these raiders were hungry enough or angry enough to risk their lives to annihilate others. Given how earliest Mankind was often evasive and ritualistic when it came to dangers from others, there must have been something worth fighting for, for the aggressors and worth defending, for those being attacked. Which means that expectations from or rights over one's home and surrounding lands had already been implanted in men's heads.

"This only became more hard wired as climactic changes took place and man learned how to gather grain, then cultivate it and also to tend animals on land. While these skills of agriculture and shepherding produced more bounty, they also resulted in man's greater dependence on specific areas of land, particularly as he lost some of his hunting and gathering skills. Without access to the land and the food and supplies that they regularly provided, the very survival of his loved ones and his clan would be at risk; thus interlopers had to be countered with any force necessary. During these 25,000 Rotations, a sense of rights and ownership became firmly grounded since even prehistoric cities were developed circa 9000 Rotations ago, with populations in the many thousands living behind walls covering scores of acres. In any situation not nearly as large there would be a hierarchy and division of labor; these earliest cities already had marked fortifications with clearly demarcated defense designs. There were walls of stone many meters thick and high, with no easy or even direct access through an outside wall into the center of the city; they had moats of amazing width and depth and even towers. Clearly by this time, war was already present. And women had become just so much property, in the final analysis.

"For many hundreds of generations, there was no need for war since land was abundant and populations were very low; these nomadic ancestors of Mankind could easily move their slash and burn activity a few miles in one direction or the other. Except at harvest time, there wasn't much to steal and even then, there was no means of transporting the booty. In short, it wasn't until there became an abundance of high value items that could easily be transported, such as stored grains or fiber or flocks of animals, that war became worthwhile as a means of stealing, at least stealing things. However, long before this, as man's dominance of women became stronger, war could be committed to obtain new women as well as slaves of both sexes.

"It took at most eighty generations to go from the first machine, the simple bow, to cities that by design, clearly indicated the presence of war. Language and the ability to communicate ever more complex ideas even if not yet in written form had to evolve over those couple of thousand Rotations to a point where extensive cooperation could occur, allowing for distinct divisions of labor and various jobs and tasks. This degree of team work resulted in early irrigation and bountiful crops as efforts were pooled; the cities themselves were built. During this time, in the millennium after the invention of the bow, the practice of sheparding began. So war eventually evolved, a highly planned effort versus the organized murders of random raiders. There was something to steal now, with cultivation at that level resulting in years of surplus; nevertheless, the domestication of horses and camels was required before a quick getaway could be possible after perpetrating large thefts. Yet a stored commodity in volume is hardly a lone prerequisite for war. While much of the world began to cultivate the land and shepherd livestock, other continents overall remained controlled by hunters and gatherers, specifically what came to be known as Australia, Africa and North America; God knows they have been warring and torturing each other it would seem since the very beginning. Which returns us to Mankind's expectations from the land he controls, with all necessary force, to enable his and his family's continued existence for the foreseeable future. Even these nomadic peoples had highly ordered societies, with appropriate cooperation as required for their daily routines. But in all of these manners of life--farming, shepherding, hunting and gathering—disagreements had to arise and had to be resolved and somebody had to make the ultimate decisions. In agricultural communities, there were priests whose perspicacity was hoped would augment annual harvests; they were the venerated ones who could command temples be built to store the grains. These temples were occupied by the priests themselves, making them the effective owners of the grain. In pastoral societies as well as the persistent hunters and gatherers, seniority was no doubt based on those traits that best aided the group as a whole. As war became a bigger concern for societies than their agricultural or pastoral basis, the theocracies gave way to top warriors who knew how to get things done.

"The shepherds became the best warriors, since they knew how to kill quickly so as not to ruin the ultimate product and disturb the herd, and they were experts at controlling crowds and recognizing animal and human leaders, that and who could be exploited.

"The first tyrants were born, having either enough food possessions or personal might to coerce others to do their bidding; to the point of being able not only to murder, but also to torture for particular emphasis to their subjects, or for their own diversion. You know there have been emperors who arranged torture for their dinner entertainment.

Water noted that he was trotting only, at this point. She had nothing to add. Now some distance from the lake, she had resumed her flight to the sea.

"The progression of torture has been relentless, the primary goal being to maximize pain and suffering; the list of types is limited only by the depravity of man's imagination and subject to the sensory design of the human body. Here man has excelled to unbelievable heights that even I would be proud of if they could be so measured. Depending on whether the torture was to extract information, punish, or be punitive and exemplary to other would be dissidents or criminals determined the length of session(s) before death if the latter was required. Coming into town over the bridge and seeing severed heads adorning spears should be a persuasive admonition to any tourist or returning resident that thou shalt do all that he has agreed to do and not infringe on his neighbors or their property. If only it was that simple. In short, woe be to the unfortunate whose criminal activity caused them to fall or who by twists of fate fell into the clutches of said tyrant, be it political, religious, or business.

Still just trotting, Water thought.

"There were the executions, simple by design, but diabolically complex in terms of the torment they would inflict, not that any death is free of fear or welcomed other than dying like a rat**, while asleep, or on some very good Drugs. Surely this was not the case for the most ancient acts of vengeance by the mob or the mob sanctioned tyrant. Imagine the sentencing options presented by this hypothetical despot to one of these pitiable souls caught in his web of doom."

I'm sure up until now you've lived a relatively normal life; thus you have had various cut fingers or other lacerations, sipped something too hot, been burned, sprained an ankle or broken a bone, gotten lint or a lash in your eye, had an injection, smashed your thumb, stubbed your toe, had a headache, gotten shocked by static or other electricity, or been overly tired. In fact, I see several old scars on your person; battle scars no doubt. These sensations, all painful, are designed to warn you of danger. But you don't know what real danger is. Fortunately for me, you were captured today and I am feeling particularly angry! So I'll review your options from this day forward, not that you're going to have many days hereafter!

With this in mind, you could be forsaken by Fire, burned alive, a fate older than the Bible itself, causing agony that will expand your last minutes into fractions of heartbeats; unleashing Fire's power, you could be burned at the stake, an appropriate demise for uncountable other enemies, the inferior, and my particular favorite for heinous crimes, witches, and heresy. You could be locked in a large, covered, dry pan, your shrieks dissipating long before your body reduces to ashes; or you could be burned in an iron box, with air holes, that is heated by a fire; or you could be boiled alive in a large pot, filled with Water, tallow, resin or oil, or fried to death over a griddle. Depending on my whim, I have had some prisoners immersed with the liquid initially at ambient temperatures, enjoying their misery as the Fire is stoked. At other times, more fun can be had by watching you writhe and scream when tossed into an already boiling cauldron. I could have you repeatedly doused with boiling Water or oil or molten lead, until your life eventually ends. Your limbs could be burned off, one at a time; or you could be slowly roasted over a small Fire, starting with your feet, your bound frame scooted up to the flames every so often; slowly roasting your whole body over an open flame has proved to allow for many hours of fiendish retribution. I could hand you over to my subjects who enjoy burning many a prisoner with torches thrust forward, movement of your bound body being limited only by the length of rope that binds your neck to a pole. Imagine the pain and destruction resulting from having a hot brand thrust into your mouth; or molten lead or boiling

Water poured down your throat or into your ears. Maybe I'll use you for a torch, lighting the night sky for my party tonight, igniting your mortal frame soaked with inflammable materials. Though I typically use this only for group punishments, the spectacle seen from the surrounding hills and the palace is most pleasing with greater numbers, especially if properly choreographed. While prehistoric in terms of origin, death by Fire has remained an acceptable means of satiating the mob's thirst for retribution. I'm sure you'd like to know that hated and feared minorities, like yourself, have been burned alive while thousands of spectators watched, not even three generations ago in the semicivilized world; I assure you, I am anything but civilized. I augur there are political and thug related executions being committed at this very moment with Fire. Regardless it hasn't been all that long ago that women, those born as life support for a vagina, would volunteer themselves to be burned alive upon the funeral pyre of their husbands, tens of thousands no less. Like a real man would want used pussy anyway.

Maybe I'll send you to the crucifixion fields with your own cross beam; I'm sure of the hundreds of stakes already in use, there is at least one on which there are only bones at this point. My men will help you take their place, properly fastening your hands and feet with nails which I prefer to rope and giving you some groin support so that the weight of your body doesn't tear the flesh and allow you to hit the ground; I can always order up some snacks with bits of food and Water, prolonging your punishment for many days. Don't like that? Well, I could have you crucified upside down, your brain being crushed by the progressive pressures that build up, long before you starve to death or die from exposure. Crucifixion was such a clever extension of our ancestor's impaling their enemies on sharpened tree trunks, leaving them left to die, don't you think?

He was obviously no longer just trotting, Water thought. Could he possibly be more glib? She showered forth past vegetation on her banks that dipped below her surface or was caught by her spray. This was truly going to be a great performance from Wind, though she wondered, how far would he go?

I have always been partial to gibbeting; the extensive misery brings me great peace over your demise. Thus I will have you hung alive or suspended, by whatever device, in a custom designed cage or by a hook inserted into a wound I will make between your ribs or abdomen. You'll be like a piece of aging meat, but still living! To be starved to death and die of thirst, over many days, exposed to the Sun and Wind and inclement weather, taunted by the locals or eaten alive by dogs.

Or maybe I'll have you broken on a cart wheel or small cross to which you can be immobilized. The executioner will smash the bones in your arms and legs with a large club or hammer, reducing your extremities to sleeves of skin like unironed shirt sleeves and pant legs, bloodied, mangled, bone and muscle, cartilage, artery and nerve fragments strewn about. You will finally be put out of your misery by a death blow to your gut, if I so choose. Otherwise, the agony lasts for days; recipients of this torture beg for a more immediate final breath. For a change of pace, I might have you draped and drawn over a barrel and then rolled downhill or over spikes.

How might you look and feel skinned alive, or having your face cut or torn off or scalped? For generations scalps have been a brutally disfiguring souvenir of battle to be traded for spoils or bounty offered by governments. Even stalwart executioners have to get into the cups for this, but I don't mind this occasional indulgence.

I could have you stoned to death by the mob, or crushed by my executioner in a giant mortar and pestle.

How about drawing and quartering? I often precede this act by having the treacherous hung half to death. While this hypoxia results in much thrashing about, your brain won't be so starved for air that you won't experience the full impact of having your limbs torn or cut apart, or otherwise mutilated before they are completely severed from your torso. This mutilation is then followed by disemboweling, cutting out your heart and ultimately decapitation, your head being placed on a pole in the public gardens.

One of my favorite variations is execution by a "thousand cuts," or so it would seem. There are so many possibilities to make this work. In one, I'll direct that a limb, or portion thereof, or just a part of your flesh is cut off each day until death results. Or the executioner can practice his art by randomly picking out hidden knives, cutting off whatever body part is named on the knife, until death is achieved by the blade of hearts. Or I can have just one dagger used, in a prescribed pattern wherein you will be dissected alive, first removing the flesh of your legs and arms, then your chest and back muscles will be sliced off a handful at a time, followed by cutting off your hair and nails, nose, ears, toes, fingers, each limb, joint by joint, up to your shoulders and hips, followed by finally thrusting the knife into your heart and then decapitation. Or maybe I'll have you stabbed over many hours in places not leading to immediate death; or maybe disemboweled and left to die; or maybe yet just gradually sawed in two. Or perhaps scraped to death with sharpened combs or wheels of razors that flay your flesh. Don't worry about premature exsanguinations; homeostasis can be controlled with judicious cautery by Fire.

I know decapitation sounds like such an easy way to go, if a violent death be your fate, which it will be. But that's only true if we use the guillotine or some other sophisticated device or I direct one of my expert swords-men, with a highly sharpened blade to be your executioner. An axe wielded by an amateur would require many hacks before achieving separation of your head from your body.

Wind was right on schedule, Water thought. She knew what was coming next. How predictable? She knew just how to pull his strings.

One of my other personal favorites, in terms of the show death puts on, struggling over your corporeal existence, comes about by Water torture. Water will drip continuously over your face or head or forcefully from an extended height. The torment from the latter is not to be believed; nor is the former ever to be forgotten by anyone who has had the pleasure of punishing or interrogating someone thusly. The gentle drops of Water will be conveyed down your throat, mouth, and nostrils via a cloth placed on your face or in your mouth, causing a feeling of and in fact drowning and choking, a horrible anguish, with all the convulsive gyrations of your heart, blood pressure, brain pressures, causing death if prolonged. On the simplistic side, when I just want to be done with a miscreant, I will have him thrown into deep Water either bound or neatly sewn into a sack with other animals, predatory or venomous. And for those foolish enough to incur my wrath, but fortunate still to catch me on a benign day, I will order near drowning with a ducking stool.

There are the mutilations without a death blow,

so that you are allowed to bleed or starve to death. This can be accomplished by throwing you from a cliff or other suitable height, crushing your bones, making you unable to move and thus starve to death for days.

I might want to suffocate you by burying you alive, either in a grave or pit covered with stones, or in a walled-in structure or box; this is one of my favorites for women.

My staff, always pushing the envelope, has devised a mechanical contraption with iron spikes that will gradually draw you ever tighter into its grasp, only enlarging the holes that pierce your flesh, observably deaf to your screams.

For a change I get satisfaction by having you dragged to death in town under public scrutiny, one leg tied to the tail of an animal or by a rope or chain threaded through holes that will be bored into your heels or hands.

Being eaten alive by starving carnivores that mangle your flesh, or fighting other condemned to the death, provides for great sport and entertainment for which my people yearn. Don't worry, you'll be closely guarded, avoiding any possibility of your suicide or inopportune death at the hands of your inmates. Maybe you can become fodder for the serpents we keep in pits as pets.

The brevity of this next spectacle is more than outweighed by the misery that occurs; one of my genius henchmen came up with this one. By means of a basin or other constricting device, rats or a cat will be immobilized over your belly and then further put in a frenzy by heat or noise, your guts eaten alive as the wretched animal tries to escape from its confinement. A variation of this, not intended to be lethal, serves well for women and results in days of screams; whereby a non-venomous insect is secured and allowed to gnaw at the flesh of her axilla, breast, or genitalia.

For simplicity of design, there is the torture of the "two hoops;" with these two hinged hoops you will be compressed in a tight crouching posture. The horror of which can only be comprehended by understanding that this is typically limited to little more than an hour, by which time blood will be seen oozing from all your orifices and even your extremities.

I have special punishments for suspected witches, the veracity of their guilt having to be established before they can be burned at the stake. Of course, trial by cold Water works either way, effectively reducing the local population by one sordid female if she should sink and establish her innocence, or back into our clutches if she should float. This isn't nearly as prolonged as directing the prickers to do their work; these artisans of sorts examine the potential sorceress's body for a sign of the devil, an area of skin that doesn't bleed or feel pain. A positive sign is elicited by poking her with long needles all over her body. Eventually, from sheer stress and shock, the victim is simply no longer able to cry out from pain related to the nth needle. There exist prickers by profession who travel from town to town, whom I can hire when needed to examine various women of the community. While they get paid by the conviction, I am confident they would never resort to trick needles that won't draw blood; I have often wondered what they did before their current crafts.

Maybe I should just maim and not kill you, leaving you alive with a constant reminder of your perfidy. I typically defer this for the folks whose peccadilloes I find irritating, but otherwise not personally threatening. These would be the mutilations, not lethal, or at least not planned as such; my executioners try to check their enthusiasm at the dungeon door, but human frailty cannot always be predicted; such is life. Still, these consist of the destruction of one or more of your body parts. The quickest, but by no means the best in terms of longevity of torment, are the amputations; accordingly, I might castrate you or have one or more of your hands or feet cut off; or your nose or tongue or ear(s), lips, breast(s), nipple(s); or your eyes plucked or gouged out and for added anguish, hot embers placed in the empty sockets. Your fingers or other parts of your extremities can be destroyed by Fire directly or with the body part immobilized in an iron boot or glove, making for a more localized cook off. Speaking of which, these devices can also be used to melt the flesh to the bone if boiling Water, resin or other hot liquid is poured into a shoe or glove designed for such torture; other iron shoes can simply be heated and sear the flesh off when placed over the otherwise defenseless little foot. Other foot coverings or splints are available which allow spaces, admittedly small ones, for placing a wedge which can be hammered down, lacerating the muscles and splintering the bones. Or, if these are all being used, I suspect the thumbscrews might give you pause for reflection; or your teeth can be extracted with pliers or hammered out. Your arms and legs can be bound together, or just your thumbs, with tight cords or wires. By heating the latter first, wrapping the arm or leg, and then rapidly cooling the metal that is burning into your flesh, the constriction of the poor arm or leg will be sufficient to make sure that this flesh is never purposefully used again. Screws can be used to shatter bones like your heel in a boot designed with thumbscrews in mind. You could be branded on the face with a letter that declares your crime or with the seal of the state. Maybe I won't castrate you, just burn your nuts off or rupture you with prolonged pressure on your groin from sitting with a support between your legs and weights attached

> to both feet. Your tongue could be bored through with a hot poker, allowing for it to then be hooked or tied to your cheek after a hole is made there as well. I could force you to kneel on sharpened surfaces with heavy stones set upon the backs of your knees; or I could have gradually tightening cords placed on an arm or leg; care must be exercised here since too many extremities being com-pressed for too long will result in death. I might have daggers thrust into the soles of your feet or ears or have you shod like a horse; maybe I'll have your nails torn off with hot pliers and iron nails then hammered through the bleeding tissue. Bound fingers or extremities can also be crushed with wedges hammered between them; and a vice of any type, wooden or metal, can quickly render a testicle, breast, hand, foot, nose, ear of no use whatsoever, with a lifetime of pain in the process. Lastly, but by no means finally, your torturer could contort your body with bindings, think leg bound to neck or neck bound to feet, for hours at a time as he then uses your body for his chair.

Water's course had remained clear for some time now. She was enjoying her interaction with Earth below her and she was listening to Wind, too. Despite his machine-gun delivery, she really had nothing to say at this point, not wanting to interrupt this rant. Quite the contrary, she knew her silence would only escalate his seething.

> Maybe I should kill you, after all, with one of the more imaginative ways to wreak death upon a miserable soul, some quick, some less so. Imagine your face and head after igniting a small bag of gunpowder in your mouth. Or your skull ever so gradually crushed by having a small stone placed on top of your head to which progressively heavier stones are overlaid, all bound by a cord. I'll leave your skull intact and just crush your brain by

hanging you by your heels until dead, pooling blood causing excruciating torment for several days. I'll have you hung upside down with chili forced into your nose and your waist tightly bound by a cord. You can die miserably, forced to over drink and then having your penis ligated, preventing forever further urination; actually, your dick will fall off long before you die from uremia. Your skin can be fried by exposure to the hot sun for hours at a time, without protective clothing or rest. The life can literally be crushed from you as ever larger stones are laid on your chest or abdomen. Powdered glass can be shoved up your ass, lacerating the mucosa, resulting in an agonizingly long and painful demise. You might be bricked up with only your head exposed for birds and other predators to eat. I might have you tied to a tree with honey smeared on your face to attract red ants. Your hair could be tied to another criminal's. I could have you sewn into a fresh animal skin and exposed to the sun where the hide will rapidly contract, simultaneously crushing you as your flesh is abraded, these being the final events, not suffocation.

However, I am feeling beneficent; so I'm really not sure I want yet to kill you, at least not intentionally, but you do need to suffer. Perhaps you will mend your previous errors if I dislocate many of your joints; the rack naturally will do this, but my personal favorite is squassation, with your body jarred apart with the aid of a pulley, a rope, and some extra weights. I have never seen the advantage of having you lie down while the executioner works. Plus, the rack is more of a gradual torment versus the abrupt pressures that can be brought to bear by hoisting you up on a hook attached to your hands, tightly bound behind your back. Then you will drop suddenly, the added weights attached to your feet aiding gravity's effort; this can be repeated over and over again until you have passed out. The lacerations to your wrists or other joints to which the hook is attached usually expose bone. While I've never gotten around to this one, I have been told that suspending you by your thumbs and big toes over a serrated surface can be amusing; if properly planned, the point of attachment can include your genitals, of course.

Regardless of your ultimate type and timing of death, the one thing you can be sure of is that I will have you flogged; too bad that this is often fatal for many. The instruments of flagellation are like dildos, of so many varieties and types, they almost cannot be catalogued; but which include any synthetic canes or vegetation or whips variably augmented with weights of metal as heavy as lead or bone and often barbed. Flogging results in your gradually being skinned, little bits of flesh being flicked off with each crack on your back or buttocks or wherever the whip repeatedly strikes; while ten to twenty lashes generally results in fainting, more blows rapidly give way to a gelatinous blob of bleeding tissue. I have sentenced some of your compatriots to punishment so severe and prolonged that the executioner himself will become physically exhausted and have to be replaced before the sentence can be completed. If not immediate, death usually occurs within days for these unfortunate recipients; therefore, with punishment of hundreds of lashes or many more, the prisoner has had to go on the installment plan, my vengeance being extracted over many days or weeks. When my ire has been exceedingly perturbed, no creature is safe from my wrath. There have been even children whom I have ordered skinned alive; sicking my malevolent monster demons from Hell itself upon Earth, my executioners, to flog them to death. Why do I inflict such misery? Because I can! If you survive the flogging itself, I'll have your mangled wounds "treated" with salt or vinegar or other caustic agents to prevent infection. And there are those who call me inhumane! I view flogging as strictly business, not like those in the realm of the perv's perv, the sadistic floggings for means of sexual gratification or for religious penitence.

Which reminds me, want to get a woman's attention? Tether her with a string; you will be the organ grinder, she will play the monkey? Bring out the paddle. Not that you'll ever have the opportunity to find out, but you wouldn't believe what you can get a woman to do after a little paddle persuasion; we've had the damndest shows and performances. Let me tell you, a wooden paddle bored with holes approximates flogging, but with bruises that last only a few days. There is nothing like seeing a woman paddled, then perform various sexual acts, then watch her be paddled again, to the death, to put every other woman in the room on her best behavior!

When I myself go berserk, flogging a child to death isn't enough. No, when business is threatened sufficiently that I have to make this point to the lumpenpublic, which includes everyone but me, I conjure up the most fiendish torments of all: the destruction of whole families. To wit, I will order children decapitated or their heads smashed or their bodies hacked to death before their parents; or a child's back is broken and he is left to die in the fields; or a toddler is disemboweled and abandoned; or an infant is placed in a bag with a feral cat; or a pregnant woman is disemboweled, the fetus thrown to the animals, always hungry. Women are forced to hang their husbands, mothers drown their children, and daughters execute their parents. I have blinded parents and then tortured their young children in their presence for as long as the tiny bodies could survive, lasting even days. The parents obviously unable to respond to their blood curdling shrieks and tears.

On one of my more merciful days, I would order you to be pilloried. Imagine, for days at a time you would be forced to wear a board that fits around your neck or a similarly designed iron collar. At the very least this would prevent you from lying down or assuming any other posture for your head and neck; we also have models that would confine your hands, preventing you from feeding yourself as well as taking care of any other daily needs, making you entirely dependent on the kindness of family, or strangers if you have otherwise been abandoned. While pilloried, you would be paraded in the streets for the derision of your peers, this often being a good time to flog you, or amputate an ear or hand, or if the mob was totally out of control, be beaten to death by stones and vegetables and whatever else happened to be handy. Like most communities, we have multiple stocks in the square; I can't imagine a time when they would be torn down from lack of use.

It has been argued that merely repeated questioning, with lack of sleep and food, as well as threats and intimidation by my police, are forms of torture, albeit milder in scope. That is hardly a fair accusation; my police just do their jobs. Since branching out in terms of tactics, I rarely have problems with these whiners anymore, the true nature of torture having been demonstrated to them. See that head on the wall, to the right? That's one of my favorite trophies, what's left of one of my previous ministers, a relative in fact, who felt I had been a bit heavy handed. I assured him as his body was being destroyed that I wouldn't harm a hair on his head and had the taxidermists assemble by his side with the instruments of their craft so that they might begin their task as soon as death was final. I think they faithfully preserved his anguish, don't you?

While I'm deciding your fate, you'll be a resident of one of our fine prisons; these are conventional penal institutions, virtually identical to those present throughout the world until maybe five or six generations ago. I don't subscribe to the theory of reformation and gentle confinement; on the contrary, I am happy to say that in our State, prison is still torture like it is in much of the world, with vermin to tear your flesh while you sleep, unsanitary conditions wherein you can piss and crap contiguous to your bed, and little food or Water or fresh air. Sometimes, with overcrowding, there won't be enough air at all and some prisoners actually suffocate! We have singles, small cells, and cages, or ones designed with uneven sides and low ceilings. In these, which you can enjoy for a month at a time, jailer's choice, you won't be able to achieve an upright or even sitting posture. This can also be accomplished in a more traditional cell by having your ankles manacled flush to the wall in a relatively low room; I like having my prisoners tucked in at night, so plan on being chained and locked into the bed in such a way that you won't be able to move your arms or legs, let alone turn over. There will be beatings definitely, flogging (told ya!), and we might begin the betting pool again to see how many hours you can stay on the treadmill or turn the crank that does no work other than wear out your arm. Thus, while I'm cogitating, you will be little more than a slave, but without the fresh air.

I could spare your life from imminent torture and sell you into slavery. You could be stripped and auctioned to the highest bidder, along with the other slaves, regardless of gender; what happens to you after that then is of no concern to me, the buyer understanding that you can never be freed. Slavery's great! Who else will do the distasteful or humiliating tasks required by my society at no remuneration other than the minimal subsistence for life? Captured prisoners, disgruntled peasants, and unfortunate criminals like yourself are so much more useful than death or confinement would warrant. Furthermore, the regular laws, those for free citizens, don't apply. You can be chained down at night or otherwise have a cumbersome weight attached to your person; you can be branded; you can be punished at any time by your owner in any way he sees fit, without restriction, so all of the above means of torment apply and whatever else his nasty mind can inspire. Regardless of your gender, you could be fucked anytime, anyway your owner wanted; think paddle. You can otherwise be bred. You can be put to death when you're worn out, not out of euthanasia related to disease or infirmity, but for the strict purpose of not having to be supported, an animal that no longer has any value whatsoever. This isn't the Inquisition plainly so I can't sentence you to death in the galleys, which generally would have meant being flogged to death over months or perhaps years, your existence is little more than an animal's as you are chained, rowing for twenty hours or more, being fed paltry Water and food as you labor nonstop, pissing and crapping where you sit. A minimum sentence is a few years, though often multiple life sentences. Most of the peasants around here are little more than slaves, no better than the other animals on the land. But woe be to insurgents, my greatest vengeance coming for treasonous acts. Think going berserk. I know revolutions occur, but there won't be one on my watch!

I might have you driven mad as a result of sleep deprivation. After no sleep for eight days, you won't know a vagina from a knot hole in a barrel, and you won't care.

Or I might just banish you to the Forest, naked and branded on the forehead, not to be aided in any fashion by any citizen or slave under pain of death for that person.

Too bad you weren't toughened up during your adolescence, like some of the regrettable pests who fate sends my way. I have entertained an occasional man or woman who has been an earlier initiate of genital mutilation. There have been some men who, prior to my involvement, had their flesh skewered and then ripped from their bodies until they fainted as a rite of passage or had their hands brutally racked by tight gloves filled with venomous insects, the heat being as much of an irritant as the bugs themselves. Now those people could take pain!

What? You have something to say? Not in my presence you don't. If I even think you are about to speak, I will have you silenced with an iron bridle; this will project into your mouth, preventing tongue movement and possibly lacerating your tongue and mouth depending on the design. I usually reserve this for women, but am happy to make the occasional exception for one such as yourself.

So you're probably wondering, why do I use torture; if I'm not happy with you, for whatever reason, why don't I just have you shot in the head or otherwise euthanized? Because it works! The bottom line, I don't like you. I hate and despise you. You are a threat to my existence. You are an outlier.

While I don't really give a shit one way or the other, I do listen to the masses. Or at least I did at one time. So I hate what they do not understand and cannot ignore, or which are contrary to their desires or tastes; it's just a question of identifying who the majority have found weak and despise, in whatever form that minority takes. I understand this and foment otherwise normal people to call for torture when they have been compromised, when death itself is insufficient punishment for the crime and the culprit must suffer long and severely before death thankfully comes. Opportunity strikes quite often; there is a never ending supply of scumbags; and I ultimately define scumbag. I have learned the more a danger or threat is exaggerated by my propagandists, the more horrible the punishments they will inflict on our enemies. Accordingly my authority and prestige have been maximized by turning over enemies to my subjects for retribution as they deem fit; and I have learned, the more I punish, the more powerful yet I become.

Life is tough in general; so I need to have castigations that factor in this overall indifference and callousness to human suffering. What is outlandish today can be accepted tomorrow and viewed as entertainment down the line. So I need something that is fiendish and cruel and inspires fear and trembling.

When every form of entreaty or persuasion fails, torture or the threat of torture will generally work. I don't care if they're guilty or innocent; I just want results; torture secures convictions. A visiting inquisitor once said that he could make the Pope himself confess to being a heretic after some time on the rack, and I believe him. Since the truth is what I say it is, torture is efficacious in securing the truth; and it certainly is just from where I sit. Imagine the fiction torture can induce when the victim really doesn't know what we're asking. Morals and ethics be damned. I can induce the victim to sign or confess to anything, or turn in comrades or even family. No one can be proved innocent by torture; the persecuted can always justify his actions by one set of extenuating circumstances or another. Just like I'm sure you'd like to try.

After all I have sacrifices to make to our gods; this year alone we have offered tens of thousands of captives, like yourself, common criminals, the infirm, the otherwise worthless; indeed our deities demand the same blood for transgressions that we would. We practice the one and true faith, making any nonbeliever a heretic who must either confess and convert or be extinguished. What's more, I need discipline; I need the laws to be obeyed; I demand subservience. My police want confessions. We also want information and other evidence. I won't have people thinking and acting for themselves.

Consider early Christianity. When a Roman emperor hundreds of Rotations after the Catholic church was founded vowed to stamp out Christianity entirely and murdered many tens of thousands toward this goal, the survival of the Church was hardly guaranteed. Thus, the Church took a hard stand when the chance came; insulting a clergyman could result in amputations of both feet and hands, a punishment eventually reduced to just one hand by one magnanimous Pope; God bless him! And the torture of heretics was required since these were treasonous to God who might become angry and punish all of Mankind. Then the Church codified the confiscation of property owned by heretics, making much of the Inquisition nothing more than a land grab by the prevailing authorities. Why? Because they could. Why else, but for the crime of being beautiful and young, even if Catholic, would an adolescent female be gleefully handed over to the inquisitors by her family, to this moloch to which the Catholic Church had become, to be used as a mistress for as long as the convening authority found her amusing, the babies so produced and the women themselves discarded once no longer desired, lest there be any evidence of the inquisitors' actions?

The Church, like other incipient powers, watched the mob rule, observing the desire for tortured confessions followed by burning at the stake; there had to be a heretic in their midst to account for whatever happened to be the latest local malady or twist of fate causing general despair. How else to rout out and punish in the most severe way possible, if not torture? And so the Church industrialized the process; heresy was a capital offense in the earliest days of the Church and as you just learned, the Church stipulated severe punishment even for disrespect. After the survival of the Church was clear, heretics were excommunicated. But as time went on and heretics and cults began to threaten the very existence of the Church again, because of their growing popularity, torture had to be revived; and yet the Church argued against torture in civil matters since an innocent accused would be tortured only because his innocence could not be proven. Where the Church wasn't powerful, civil authorities adopted torture as a means of dealing with all criminal situations including witnesses with conflicting opinions, often in front of one another until agreement was reached. Hell, I've tried that one; works well.

Think of the power of torture that for half a millennium, for twenty generations, an entire population was forbidden to speak their minds or criticize the Church verbally and certainly not in a written fashion without respect to their rank or civil power or wealth or even possess books condemned by the Church or even a copy of the complete set of the Ten Commandments. The official Church doctrine omitted the second commandment about worshiping graven images.

It could be argued that all punishment is torture in one manner or another. I believe that this is too broad a definition, of course, since torture really is in eyes of the victim. I have found that psychological torture can be every bit as debilitating as physical abuse, the goal being to bewilder and paralyze the recipient, affecting his ability to function as an independent human being if properly administered.

I don't mind that my state sponsored torture affects society psychologically; what I sanction individuals themselves will carry out on a limited basis engendering the aphorism, torture or be tortured. No doubt many closet sadists find their outlet by working in environments where they can surreptitiously practice their cruelty among the weak and despised, be it in the care of animals, butchery, prisons, asylums but also schools, camps, and even churches, particularly with regard to children. And those who want to go pro can always knock on our door. There are always some who have to satiate their thirst to run with the big dogs, in terms of looking for positions of power in government, and they don't care what they have to do to get or maintain it. We're always hiring.

Like in ancient times, prisoners "die while in prison" whenever the torture inadvertently proves fatal and the initial accusation would not have readily warranted such ruthlessness. Tough shit! And if the law says a virgin can't be strangled, which I find just, then I order the executioner to rape her first.

Thus you have heard a well catalogued and classically described set of abominable torments. Just the thought of all these delicious acts of barbarism makes me horny. But enough of you. What's your pleasure? Speak! I command you! While you still have a tongue in your head!

"Whew! What a GDMFSOB**?" Water had to raise her voice to be heard. This repetition did have much new material, she had noted. Wind had done his homework prior to this storm. The sandy typhoon was well underway and she was a distance yet from the ocean. She wondered how much further she could push him. The desert was dissipating as grasslands and hills began to provide Water with additional refreshments.

"You got that right," Wind belched back. "We're certainly in agreement there. The guy is a major prick, the concatenation of styles over thousands of Rotations notwithstanding. I guess for him torture is an inevitable result of war. He obviously doesn't care about genocide, but even in those societies where it is officially condemned, traitors and spies usually require the persuasion that only torture can bring to bear, this being accomplished by purported allies if necessary. In many wars, and I suspect his are included, torture is also the ultimate fate of anyone who happens to fall defenseless into the clutches of his enemy, to be disposed of as they see fit. In the worst case scenario, civilians and military slaughter each other, resulting in the quick and horrible mutilation of tens of thousands, in the lust for revenge. Thus are born the legendary reigns of terror that occur every few generations."

"But even the inquisitors, those masters of death knew their limits," Water replied. "After all, a fornicating monk would have a long chain secured to his neck through a hole bored with a hot poker. He could then be led naked around town begging for money for the monastery, being flogged by another monk behind him whenever he sought to take pressure from the chain off the wound."

"Sounds like a fitting punishment to me," Wind retorted. "Maybe they should start that again with hypocritical clergy. My, oh my, that would make a pretty picture."

While Water ignored this, she did agree with the proposition; the punishment should fit the crime. "Cultures with torture suffer reduced creativity and independent thinking since the daily threat of terrible suffering bends the concept of what is true and what is fiction. Promulgated by whatever propagandists are in power, the torture is psychological as well as physical. Excessive punishment or torture is a further crime upon the population. After all, there is the rhetorical question that if the authorities wanted such and such, they would have ordered such and such and by one's having raised an issue, they have to ask, are you questioning their wisdom or authority, and so on? If there is true freedom of thought, then the mob can never collect against any heresy."

"And nothing unites the mob or is more egalitarian than the call for vengeance, for 'self preservation,' in the war of 'us versus them;' the maxim, 'you're either with us or against us,' works well here. Isn't it a shame? Since the punishments obviously did little to dissuade people either from their beliefs or from crime; some things just can't be changed," cautioned Wind.

"Perhaps," he continued, "there is a grander plan at work concerning Mankind's overall frailty, permitting him to expire after a reasonable amount of abuse. How many healthy young men have we seen, who if they survived the ordeal, meaning that they were not murdered as part of the torture, would be transformed into withered, misshapen, deformed old men? And you remember that young woman who went to the southern continent in the western hemisphere?"

"Yes, but I don't want to," pleaded Water, as she began churning through the first of many synthetic canals, still hundreds of kilometers from the coast.

"Well, you're going to anyway!" By this point, Wind's storm consisted of a massive front of air buttressing the elements below her. Tornadoes were being spawned in all directions, wreaking havoc on the vegetation as well as many of Mankind's tools and toys left out for him to enjoy. "While there visiting, she disappeared. Her parents sought to learn of her whereabouts and were only told that she was arrested. Eventually, after long silences and hundreds of thousands of dollars spent, they were told that she was dead; that she died in prison, and she had been arrested as a spy. In good faith, her captors agreed to return her remains. A jar with a pair of hands was forwarded to her parents. In their horror, despite having hoped against hope, they couldn't deny that these hands indeed looked like their daughter's.

"And we both also know that this is but one example of everyday, everywhere occurrences, which extrapolates the figures into what? Hundreds of millions, beyond question, perhaps billions, if one includes war, crime, persecution, abuse of women and children. How can their collective agony possibly be understood or measured? Perhaps, dear Water, their tears are manifest in your very oceans."

"I have certainly shared the agony of my children, my loved ones," began crashing Water, spilling from her banks into low lands occupied by all kinds of Species, including humans. "And have been loathe ever to be used in the misery of any human. Like with Fire, Mankind likes to think he can control me and tries at times to place limits around me. His grander efforts are generally useless trifles."

"What with monarchs sacrificing their own children in years gone by, it's a wonder Mankind has managed to get as far as he has. What's most frightening is that most of these torments are still in use today, all over Earth and now supplemented by electric shock, Drugs, brainwashing; gas and liquid fed torches and smoking materials, matches and lighters obviating the need for open Fires. Probably all, no matter how incomprehensible, have been used at one time or another by all of the legendary tyrants in the last few generations, tens of millions being exterminated through torture and genocide. Religious fervor that requires any other person with opposing views to be exterminated, minimized, or punished in any way should be the 8th deadly sin, since the millions upon millions slaughtered related to religion in one fashion or another would make God Almighty, Himself, question His own Existence. But it goes on, it never stops, martyrs on the short list, the executioners on the long. Or should it be the other way around?"

Not wishing to solve his riddle for him, Water mused, "The way to stop torture is through the state avoiding any corporal punishment of any type and by embracing democracy of thought. Children should have pets with supervised, humanitarian training of proper pet care. Crime should be punished according to the individual, not the crime."

"You mean the state should ask the criminal what would he would regard as reasonable punishment? As if!"

"Not exactly. But as the tyrant noted, what is inhumane to one person is a picnic and a day off from work for another. If the state could determine what the criminal holds dear, perhaps he could be punished more appropriately. Nevertheless, the punishment is just part of the problem, very few states work on reformation of their criminals." Water further thought to herself that most villains were indeed victims of circumstances, that this might really work in the right State, and that all but a few of the incorrigibles are redeemable; but she didn't say this to Wind in their discussion which she regarded as academic at best. He had started it, she recalled; she had been peacefully meditating.

Not to be outdone, Water gushed forth, "But look how advanced Mankind is becoming with all of his technology; he has advanced medical capabilities and food production, transportation and communication, manufacturing and pleasure." The fields, towns, and forests were flooding further with her increasing ire and Wind was whipping her in all directions.

"Your affection for Mankind is clouding your judgment, dear Water. What has technology ever been for Mankind other than a means of having an edge over other humans who do not? In order to subjugate them in one manner or another, either by force of destruction, with death, or by information; either propaganda or lack of independent sources, which is a variant of subterfuge or brainwashing when carried to the extreme.

"What is technology but first the means of war and domination, always being one up on the competition in terms of one's weapons? Now there is a word that should never have been invented in any language, a weapon meaning literally, any device or construct used for fighting. That definition refers to the singular which doesn't sound too barbaric since there are multiple types of fighting; but when it becomes plural, there is a sinister ascendancy that takes hold, at once denoting aggression. Perhaps there is the sense of equity at stake here, meaning that everyone is allowed to have a weapon for protection; but when a body has more than one, it is not only not fair, it suggests that he has a purpose other than self preservation. Though perhaps he is paranoid or involved in work where he should be.

"Again let's look to where Mankind started," he went on. "Weapons were relatively slow to advance in the earliest stages, their progression was far more logarithmic than linear. As long as 100,000 Rotations ago Mankind's ancestors had already learned to fix flint or stone onto a handle to augment a blow at close range. These could be used for all kinds of domestic chores as well as smashing the body or head of an enemy, animal or human. Such tasks could be considered just so much of the daily routine in terms of protection, providing meat and other raw materials for augmenting lifestyle.

"By 40,000 Rotations ago, Homo sapiens was clearly present; his weapon of choice was the spear. About 10,000 Rotations ago, marking the new stone age, the simple bow became known, quite possibly the earliest appliance. Man could for the first time distance himself from a kill, no longer having to be physically present at arm's length. While the dagger followed from the spear head, the sling from bolas, and the mace from a club, each of these still required far more personal risk than the bow afforded. The polished stone axe allowed slash and burn; we saw shepherding at least 9000 Rotations ago. Probably 7000 Rotations ago bullocks were being used for carrying and pulling. Bear in mind that all this time, flint needed to be worked and mined. The first complex metallurgy occurred perhaps 6000 Rotations ago and so copper which had long been fashioned became bronze with tin; but both of these were relatively scarce resources, particularly the tin. Still from this primitive industry came the first emperor as technology advanced the science of smelting, alloying, and casting. The first use was the socket axe, consisting of a metal blade securely riveted into a wooden handle.

"The composite bow, perhaps fifty times stronger than the simple bow, first appeared about 5000 Rotations ago. But forty generations were required to perfect the technology of gluing wood together followed by prolonged, artful steaming, curving, and gluing of the central grip and tips. Undoubtedly the pastoralists perfected the composite bow and ultimately the chariot, finding that these were useful for protecting herds from predators and allowing them to keep up with their flocks. They were now able to move faster by an order of magnitude. Eventually horses of sufficient strength and size were bred and war began in earnest. For some, the steppe peoples, war became their way of life, taking the spoils and women, a few slaves, and killing the rest."

Water was impervious to his blasts, being malleable just short of her atomic components. Was he ever lit now? she thought. Was she good or was she great?

"Fortifications for refuge, strongholds, and strategic defenses if necessary were the only answers the farmer could devise to counter the horse breeders living on the fringes. Once well provisioned, these were virtually impenetrable, being both a defense and a point of defiance to central authority.

"Some 4300 Rotations ago iron extended metals to the masses, no longer the exclusive province of the well to do, those who could afford the copper and tin required for bronze. Quite possibly the secret of iron was very well guarded for 1000 Rotations, but more likely, many generations were required for production of a proper furnace and the forced draught of a bellows rather than Wind. Moreover, at least some nickel was required, hardly obvious, and iron required finishing with hot hammering and quenching rather than cold hammering that worked so well for bronze. I suspect the smelting of iron was a serendipitous finding; but over a 1000 Rotations, chance has plenty of time to strike. Regardless, iron allowed standardization and the ability to make machines to make machines, increasing output. This meant that armies could be much larger in terms of outfitting them including armor and mail.

"Logistics, ever important since the first general, prompted Roman engineers to build roads and canals.

"Coils and weight bearing devices such as catapults were only so effective against high walls that were closely guarded. And so the composite bow, requiring centuries for perfection, once done, did not change again as the chief weapon until gun powder was perfected for weaponry about 500 Rotations ago. The crossbow, while more mechanical than its much older brother, was still no match.

"With the use of gunpowder, walls and armor, so highly valued at the time, became penetrable. Gunpowder allowed a projectile to be sent forth in a straight trajectory at the wall's foundation and it greatly increased the force of assault in a controlled manner and at an even greater distance. First used ceremonially in China about 1000 Rotations ago, and probably discovered by alchemists in Europe much later, gunpowder required seven generations of engineers and scientists to make firearms highly mobile, both on land and sea, as well as hand held.

"Gunpowder's supremacy in siege was checked in just two generations. That was all that was required to redesign city walls as low fortified, sloping bastions to best resist cannon fire, a completely different design than the tall walls that had marked castlization for many centuries. But despite gunpowder's invention, for hundreds of Rotations, it was a high value item since one of the ingredients was difficult to find in bulk.

"The technology of the last six to eight generations allowed murder by war on a massive scale. Chemists found ways to mass produce potassium nitrate and this was followed by other chemical explosives, think TNT. Physics, chemistry, and engineering advanced the science of the cannon, the projectile, and the personal weapon. The steam engine allowed for railroads and the sailing of ships that no longer required the whims of Wind or galleys of slaves for propulsion. Peaceful uses, of course; but critical for waging and winning war.

"And all of these were greatly advanced by the introduction of steel a mere 150 Rotations ago. But the steel industry needed something to do with their vast output; buildings could only be so high without elevators. There could be only so many trains, tracks, and bridges; the automobile wasn't yet on the scene in numbers that made a difference. The obvious solution was supplying the gargantuan military buildup that culminated in the global conflicts. Wasn't it fortuitous that the industrialists were able to advance their wares to accommodate the increasingly nationalistic rhetoric that took hold in those days, forming an especially poignant amalgam of government and capitalism at its worst?"

Water tried to speak up. They were now near the shore. The mudslides, flooding, and overall damage would prove to be legendary in Mankind's calendar. She raised her voice even further, but was again drowned out by Wind.

"While cannon foundries have always remained under government control, personal weapons have been available to the mob from the very beginning. A different arms race was on once these could be manufactured by standardized components; each manufacturer trying to design a rifle or handgun that was slightly better than the competition's, resulting ultimately in the revolver, machine gun, and automatic weapons, with distance, accuracy, portability, and load and firing power being the variables to be maximized.

"Political and social sciences also advanced, building on much of the Romans' forgotten talents. Armies were now being formed with officers, not noblemen in charge. Citizen recruits were highly trained, drilled, and equipped with the most advanced weapons. No longer were men just following their leader.

"Bullocks finally gave way as the singular means of supply, after nearly 7000 Rotations, with the invention of petroleum based engines. Feeding of troops required canning meat, evaporating and drying milk, and inventing margarine. Tanks checked nearby firepower. Industrialization led to the exponential production of weapons and logistical supports and the fabrication of their increasingly consumed raw materials. And so there came submarines, airplanes, and missiles, each with a counter measure being devised fairly quickly. How many tens of thousands of rounds must be spewed to stop reliably a missile traveling faster than the speed of sound? Now that's technology! But there are also satellites and computers and codes; mathematics and the physical sciences have brought Earth atomic weapons. Sure, atomic energy is used for civilian power supplies; but which came first, bombs or power stations?

"While technology has generally split weapons into either the offensive or defensive moiety, atomic weapons could never be argued to be a means of defense other than through détente. They represent the current culmination of Mankind's search for the maximum bang for his buck, gram for gram; and they are easily stored and delivered.

"Even before nuclear weapons were invented, Mankind had unleashed chemical agents; God are they are devastating. And now even the biologic sciences are getting into the act.

"The primary goal is always to kill the enemy at as much a distance as possible. Ideally the soldier and his loved ones are completely safe either from his weapon or theirs; preferably at the push of a button. What could be simpler? What could future weapons possibly offer that isn't available now, short of the complete preservation of any infrastructure and the ability to exterminate only that part of the population truly in opposition? But that's available now; it's called assassination and it is probably undergoing as much scrutiny today as it ever was. Too bad the enemy can't just be willed to death! Probably someone is working on that as well."

Wind was approaching cyclotronic speeds, threatening to annihilate the silicon in the beach sand with other silicon. "Even history has its place in planning and executing war. Unfortunately, the last war is always fought first in any new conflict. Worse yet, the lens used to divine

Mankind's earlier follies is always warped. Thus, this time it's different, forever applies. But toward this goal, men actually have war colleges: this is how we kill our enemies. And while torture is surely not taught in any reputable war college, how else can the apprentice learn his abominable craft but through see one, do one, teach one."

"Enough already!" thundered Water, her clouds of vapor shooting bolts of lightning in the air followed by terrific cracks. Even Wind was momentarily stunned and immediately began to quiet down. "I for one didn't have to hear about all this again, not needing your homily. I am well aware of Mankind's foibles, entirely meant as a diminutive. He is after all Homo sapiens; however, he still hasn't entirely mastered Fire.

"And as far as our Bet is concerned," Water gently went on, "I'm not the least bit worried. Despite there being a gargantuan number of scumbags, Mankind will survive. I have seen to it."

"Within our rules?"

"Roger that." She was becoming more playful again. The Sun was visible again in the sky between the dark clouds that were being swept to sea through Wind's custodial efforts.

"You're bluffing."

"Bullshit! Just watch."

* * * * * * * * * *

AND NOW, IT'S time for a message from the sponsors:

BlahblahblahBlahblahblahBlahSexBlahblahblahBlahblahblahBlahBlahblahblahBlahblahblahBlahBlahblahblahBlahblahblahBlahBlahblahblahChocolateBlahblahblahBlahBlahblahblahBlahblahblahBlahBlahblahblahBlahblahblahBlahBlahblahblahBlahblahblahBlahBlahblahblahBlahblahblahBlahBlahblahblahBlahblahblahBlahBlahblahblahBlahblahblahBlahBlahblahblahBlahblahblahBlahBlahblahblahBlahblahblahBlahPussyBlahblahblahBlahblahblahBlahBlahblahblahBlahblahblahBlahBlahblahblahBlahblahblahBlahBlahblahblahBlahblahblahBlahBlahblahblahBlahblahblahBlahBlahblahblahBlahblahblahBlah

BlahblahblahBlahblahPainreliefblahBlahBlahblahblahBlah
blahblahBlahBlahblahblahBlahblahblahBlahBlahblahblah
BlahblahblahBlahBlahblahblahBlahblahblahBlahBlahblah
CleavageblahBlahblahblahBlahBlahblahblahBlahblahblah
BlahBlahblahblahBlahblahblahBlahBlahblahblahBlahblah
blahBlahBlahblahblahBlahblahblahBlahBlahblahblahBlah
blahblahBlahBlahblahblahBlahblahblahBlahBlahblahblah
BlahblahblahBlahBlahPersonalhygieneblahblahBlahblahbl
ahBlahBlahblahblahBlahblahblahBlahBlahblahblahBlahbl
ahblahBlahBlahblahblahFoodBlahblahblahSexBlahBlahbla
hblahBlahblahblahBlahBlahblahblahBlahblahblahBlahBla
hblahblahBlahblahblahBlahBlahblahblahBlahblahblahBlah
BlahblahblahBlahblahblahBlahBlahblahblahBlahblahObesi
tyblahBlahBlahblahblahBlahblahblahBlahBlahblahblahBla
hblahblahBlahBlahblahblahBlahblahblahBlahBlahblahblah
BlahblahblahBlahBlahblahblahBlahblahblahBlahBlahblah
blahBlahDrugsblahblahBlahBlahblahblahBlahblahblahBla
hBlahblahblahBlahblahblahBlahBlahblahblahBlahblahblah
BlahDepressionBlahblahblahBlahSexblahblahBlahBlahbla
hBeautyaidsblahBlahblahblahBlahBlahblahblahBlahblahbl
ahBlahBlahblahblahBlahblahblahBlahBlahblahblahBlahbl
ahCommunicationblahBlahBlahblahblahSexBlahblahblahB
lahBlahblahblahBlahblahblahBlahBlahblahblahBlahblahbl
ahBlahBlahblahblahBlahblahblahFoodBlahBlahblahblahSe
xBlahblahblahBlahBlahFoodblahblahBlahblahblahSexBlah
BlahblahblahBlahblahblahBlahBlahblahFoodblahBlahblah
blahBlahBlahblahblahBlahblahblahBlahSexBlahblahblahBl
ahblahblahBlahBlahblahblahBlahblahblahBlahBlahblahbla
hBlahblahblahBlahBlahblahblahBlahblahblahBlahBlahbla
hblahBlahblahblahBlahBlahblahblahBlahblahblahBlahBiki
niBlahblahblahBlahMoneyblahblahBlahBlahFoodblahblah
BlahblahblahBlahBlahblahblahBlahblahblahBlahBlahblah
blahBlahblahblahBlahBlahblahblahBlahblahblahBlahBlah
blahblahBlahblahblahBlahBlahblahblahBlahSexblahblahBl
ahBlahblahblahBlahblahblahBlahBlahblahblahBlahblahbla
hBlahBlahblahblahBlahblahblahBlahBlahSexblahblahBlah
blahblahBlahBlahblahblahBlahblahblahBlahBlahblahblah
BlahblahblahBlahBlahblahblahBlahblahblahBlahBlahblah
blahBlahblahblahBlahBlahblahblahBlahblahblahBlahBlah

blahblahBlahblahblahBlahBlahblahblahBlahblahblahBlahBlahblahblahBlahFoodblahblahBlahBlahPetsblahblahBlahblahblahFoodBlahBlahblahblahBlahblahblahBlahBlahblahblahBlahblahblahBlahBlahblahblahBlahSexblahblahBlahBlahblahblahBlahblahblahBlahBlahblahblahBlahblahblahBlahBlahblahblahBlahblahblahBlahBlahFoodblahblahBlahblahblahSexBlahBlahblahblahBlahblahblahFoodBlahBlahblahblahBlahblahblahSexBlahBlahblahblahBlahblahblahBlahSexBlahblahblahBlahblahblahBlahBlahblahblahChocolateBlahblahblahBlahBlahblahblahFoodBlahblahblahBlahBlahblahblahBlahblahblahBlahBlahblahblahBlahblahblahBlahBlahblahblahBlahblahblahBlahBlahSexblahblahBlahblahblahBlahBlahblahblahBlahblahSexblahBlahBlahblahblahBlahblahblahBlahFoodBlahblahblahBlahblahblahBlahBlahblahblahBlahblahblahBlahBlahblahblahBlahblahblahBlahBlahblahblahBlahFoodblahblahBlahBlahblahblahBlahblahblahSexBlahBlahblahblahBlahblahblahBlahBlahDeoderizersblahblahBlahFoodblahblahBlahBlahblahSexblahBlahblahblahBlahBlahblahblahBlahblahblahBlahBlahblahBlah

# Book 7 Adolescent

"MULE EYEBROWS..." That's all you hear, the words ricocheting inside your skull. You sit there momentarily stunned. You've never heard that mispronunciation before. Your ears singe again, as you start to get up, "Mule eyebrows..." The PCD in your pocket starts to buzz; as you continue walking to room 37, you pull it out of your pocket, preparing to message back the office that you're on your way. The Registrar's office will be ready for you soon, you assume. Your attention has certainly been side tracked, but you quickly notice that everyone's PCD is yelping and there are three flashing red lights on huge screens at the center of the Registrar's Rotunda. Each projects 120 degrees.

You look around and see everyone literally stop where they are. Your PCD folds open and also sports the triple red warning, both on the cover in case you had just glanced at it; but in this instance the salutation forces the contraption open, placing in your hand an eight by twelve by one-eighth inch monitor where a six square inch device had originally been. You look down into your hands and then again into the Rotunda; the messages are identical; you see the same pattern on other people's screens.

This has never before happened in your lifetime. Your history lessons had taught that the last time there was a general declaration of urgent magnitude from the Minister's office was over 400 Rotations ago.

Your curiosity doesn't have to wait long. Within moments Minister Esse is broadcasting to all CDs everywhere there are human beings. "All Eartherians, I beseech your attention and consideration. Just minutes ago I spoke with an Alien species here on Earth! They landed within a few blocks of the Ministerial Mansion. They have told me they wish to address all Eartherians. So that everyone can have time to fulfill or set aside immediate obligations, we plan to hold our conference in six hours. Please tidy up your days or evenings in a timely fashion and plan accordingly. This communication will repeat every thirty minutes, until acknowledged by you; after that your CDs will regain full function as before, up until the time of the broadcast itself."

The screens then return to their defaults and your PCD prepares to fold up. You let the Office know you are coming first, their request being the second in the queue; you were right after all.

Arriving on the other side of the columned facility, you introduce yourself at the counter. "Ma'am, I'm Muliebris ...," which you pronounce as four distinct syllables, mu-li-e-bris, 'mu' like the Greek letter not the cow, 'lee,' the 'e' being pronounced as a long 'a,' and all the letters in 'bris' are pronounced, with a short 'i'. "My friends call me Mu," you say.

While listening to the Registrar talk about your schedule and placement scores, you can't help but think, where on Earth had your parents come up with this name? But they were eccentric at times, even for your Society. Your mind momentarily returns to a game in class when you were eight. The teacher had everyone play a game wherein the students came up with the first associations regarding everyone's names including the teacher's. There was no anger, no tears, no embarrassment; there was plenty of outrageous laughter and honesty of opinion, you grew to realize. You giggle a little and smile, recalling how fun that game had been and how it had taught you early on to think from a different perspective.

The Registrar mistakes your lightheartedness for enthusiasm, which is nonetheless present. "Mu, you need one more essay to place into an advanced class. You will have three days, since time is a factor in this particular area of study."

Suppressing your grimace, but with some flush to your cheeks, you say without fawning, "Thank you for your time, Ma'am. Good-bye, until the fall. The essay will be forthcoming."

You walk back to the shuttle depot, one coming every fifteen minutes. On the way you speak first with your father, via your PCD, who is at his lab, a few miles down the road from your home and then with your mother who is shopping. They assure you they are fine and plan to be back home prior to Minister Esse's conference with the Aliens.

"We trust in Minister Esse's judgment," your mother says. "What are you going to write the additional essay about?" she asks, clearly convinced life will go on.

"I'm not sure," you mumble, displeased that there is one more hurdle for you prior to this class. "It is an upper level course. Maybe I'm biting off more than I can chew," you wonder to her.

"I doubt that. What are the basic requirements?"

"It has to be about something I have never researched before; moreover, I am not allowed to do any specific investigation for this. I think they want to see what I can do with my general knowledge to date."

"So it would seem. You've had many experiences, darling, and your reading is extensive for your age. Recall our excursions and the wondrous museums we've visited. Surely there are a surfeit of topics you could pick. Do some thinking on your way home this afternoon. Get lunch on the transport and let your mind relax. It will come to you."

"OK, Mama, I will. I love you."

"I love you, too. By the way, your hair is making progress. The complete curls shouldn't take much longer. See you soon. Bye-bye."

On the transport home to Omaha, from Geneva, you have an avocado and muenster cheese sandwich, with a few sprouts, on whole grain bread. To drink you have Water that is carbonated and sweet, but not fattening (of course). You settle in your seat, close your eyes and begin thinking about the day.

You will be attending University in the fall, away from your family for the first time for any extended duration, and will study art; specifically photography, which you define as any illustration taken through the interpretation of a lens, subject to optically mandated laws of imaging, and subsequently processed to any degree whatsoever, or not at all. This is to be distinguished from graphic design which can render any image that the imagination can engender, but is otherwise not real, other than in terms of 1s and 0s. Now graphic design can make for brilliant art, but it is not photography as it has always been; anyone can make any motif with a computer and the right software, you think. Images in binary exist only in cyberspace, if not first folded by a lens, but to be fair, you acknowledge the existence of light sensitive digital transducers that can not only mimic the visual perspective of humans, but multiple animal species. The final rendition being the further transformed image as seen through a lens of variable focal length. Regardless, you are particularly interested in multidimensional photographs, but not the holographic images which are an easy option for displaying one's work; and certainly not anything that is digitally altered in any fashion, since that would merely constitute a variant of graphic design. You have some ideas about how this might be accomplished, but are still working on many of the details in your head. You would of course continue to take a general smattering of other subjects, the purpose of your education at this point being to provide four things: to teach you how to think critically, to provide you with a general data base and the ability to continue learning things on your own, and to enrich you with an in-depth experience in one particular realm.

You arrive home a few hours later. Your family lives in a farming community that grows corn and wheat professionally, most everyone cultivating a small garden for vegetables that their family enjoys throughout the seasons. You walk up the curved stairs, which are broader at the base and open below; nevertheless, the stairs themselves are solid, without any openings that could catch your foot. You smile as you climb the stairs to your room, many fond memories coming to mind as you think about past playtime under the stairs.

Your room is about twenty by thirty feet, not very big. In addition to your queen size bed, a four poster, there is your desk, a four by six feet surface that folds down from the wall when not in use, which is rare, since you often use it for photographic experiments as well as your lessons. Like all bedrooms and the kitchen, the closet also houses a recycling box. One wall consists of the huge DCD that is present in each main room of the house. You place your PCD on the desk and sit down, scooting your chair on castors to a comfortable distance. You grasp your camera bag and gently extract each lens; you only use two or three with any regularity. There is your wide angle, which increases depth of field and accentuates the central object with little distortion, and your telephoto, which does the opposite but allows tight framing with amazing clarity. You turn these over in your hands as you think about your experience at the double R, the euphemism for the Registrar's Rotunda in Geneva. You also glance around the room, the walls painted a sweet, pale blue, like the sky itself. On other walls you have displayed some of your art. Your favorites are the still-lifes, the panoramic landscapes, and the animals.

Your photographs adorn other walls throughout the house, in addition to paintings and Water colors, to name a few of the genres that your parents like to collect. You recall many mornings of waking up early and scanning locations in order to find just the right time when the ambient light would be perfect; your commitment is manifest in the quality of the awards that emboss your home as well. Photography will, evidently, be just your initial career after college. How many professions will you have in your lifetime, you wonder? As with everything else in your Society, currently presided over by Minister Esse, there are no set rules.

Minister Esse is the final arbiter over all Eartherian controversies, and you mean the planet and Species, not the language. This has been the way of your Society for many generations, since the Plague anyway. She has held three terms which, while not unprecedented, has not occurred for at least 200 Rotations, each term being fifteen Rotations. As brilliant as she is, even Minister Esse would not set forth any specific conventions about leading one's life.

You may not want to pursue photography anyways after college; it is not uncommon to learn just enough about one subject in six Rotations that the student never wants to hear about it again. Some things never change, you think, recalling how reviews of ancient statistics in education bore this out 1000s of Rotations ago.

Nature calls and you relieve yourself in your bathroom, there being one in each bedroom. You're still trying to think about a topic for the essay.

You look out the window and see the bountiful crops communing with the Earth and Wind; each a dot in the medley of the landscape. You also gaze for a moment at the gazebo and a portion of your brain thinks of your boyfriend. Your yard has no fence, nor do your neighbors; their horses occasionally come over and visit. They are such powerful creatures, you think, but never sport for riding. Clouds meld and are reborn by Wind's lackadaisical kneading.

The DCD in your room and those elsewhere in the house have returned to the defaults or the screens in use prior to Minister Esse's proclamation; obviously your parents acknowledged the message as well. As you walk downstairs, you see Manet's Bar at the Folies-Bergerie prominently displayed on the opposing wall, a masterful piece that brings you continuous joy as you observe meticulous detail. The bright, direct light on the bar maid clearly delineates her no-two-ways-about-it demeanor; the rest of the painting consists entirely of objects and a gentleman customer reflected in the mirror behind her, the latter intriguingly at an angle to her.

This wing of the downstairs is a square sixty feet by sixty feet, with vaulted ceilings and exposed beams. Two sides consist of glass that extend from the floor to at least twenty feet high. Via the furnishings, your parents have divided the room into multiple smaller sections for intimate gatherings, from informal to quite stuffy.

You have a seat on one of the couches, staring outside with one eye and at the DCD with another; which means that you are really looking at nothing. The essay remains on your mind, of course; but your concentration is also juxtaposed to Minister Esse's pending interview with real live Aliens, here on Earth! With the breakthrough of ISDs, some 500 Rotations ago, Mankind has visited thousands of worlds, with hundreds inhabited by sentient beings, but none nearly capable of interstellar travel; many were quite hostile and fearful. With each passing generation after space travel began, the statisticians continued to define the probability of discovering other Species as advanced or perhaps more so than Mankind. After awhile the number continued to slope towards zero. They were never found. This had always caused Society some consternation and given rise to considerable speculation at all levels. Nevertheless, your approach to one another and different Species less technologically advanced has been unchanged. There is tolerance and enlightenment at all levels.

You take this for granted, unquestionably. How could people possibly function in any other way? How can you comprehend the horror of life on Earth before the Plague? You have read about and spoken with people who have visited less hospitable worlds. While they have always been safe, their observations and vignettes highlight rituals, cruelty, insensitivity and despair, despite many otherwise redeeming features. These were all Alien cultures, however, not human.

While detailed records have been available for 1000s of Rotations, giving a great perspective on the progression of civilization, it is difficult for you to imagine life prior to the Plague. Despite the longevity of human life now, there have not been survivors of the Plague for at least several generations.

The essay. Your mind remains a blank. On the DCD you

display messages and see one from your closest friend, Jizelle. You contact her via your DCD. “Hi Jizelle. You look very busy.” As she comes on, she tells you she is juggling at least three other conversations. Her interests include statistics and probability theory.

“Hey, Mu! Yeah, what a day? How’s it going? Your curls are coming along nicely.”

“Yeah, I like your hair, too; the blond coloring is starting to shimmer.”

“Thanks, Mu. How was registration?

“Fine,” which it was other than the bastardization of your name, which you don’t mention, and the need for the additional essay, which you do.

“That’s going to be tough,” Jizelle admits. “You’ll think of something,” she goes on. “Let your mind grope for the most basic concepts of life if possible. Think simply. On a different note, I have been in touch with some of my friends in statistics. Their conclusion about Minister Esse’s announcement is that it’s improbable, but quite possibly true, wondering if this is a hoax. But prank or not, as you know, Aliens have never been seen on Earth, unfriendly or otherwise and we have been traveling the Heavens for over 500 Rotations!”

“No shit. I think it is for real.”

“Me, too. Hey, assuming we’re still in existence next week,” and she laughs, “are we still on for our outing?”

“Af-fir-ma-tive,” is your monotonal answer, which you can’t sustain for more than a brief last syllable, before breaking up and laughing, too.

“Don’t give me that bullshit,” Jizelle continues, beginning to laugh so hard she says her cheeks are hurting.

“Whoa,” you get out, between puffs, grabbing your thighs with your hands and taking slow breaths. “Yeah, I’m hot to go to Amsterdam next week. We can be there in just over ninety minutes by transport. I want to go to that great café we found last month. We can get completely shit-faced, and then gorge ourselves with the cheese and bread. And for dessert we can have crème brulee, chocolate or coffee, and ice coffee.”

"Sounds great to me. Got to go. Bye."

"Right. Bye, Jizelle," you say as she signs off. She certainly is hyper today, you think. On the DCD you look over your schedule for this week and next week, marking the day that the essay is due.

You then look over your calendar from the last few weeks, and note your visit to the pre-Plague Museum in North America which, by transport, is about a half hour from your home town. The artifacts are quite well preserved and provide great detail of life at that time. You have a sip of your drink and fidget on the couch.

You pull up your annotations from that visit. In your daily diary, you keep thoughts and conclusions, ideas and general comments on your observations. Museums of all types are essential to Society's understanding and acknowledging the past, you think. Particularly since the most you have heard first hand is your oldest living relative's recollections of conversations with their oldest living relatives. Still, despite humans living several hundred Rotations, the birth rate is such that this generally equates into one's grandparent's grandparents.

You know the history of Mankind was little changed until better means of hygiene were practiced, and industry and technology markedly improved; after that there was rapid, no, geometric growth. Surely those first generations growing up with electricity, with personal conveyance devices, rapid global travel, global communications, reliable birth control, and plentiful food, could never have imagined the daily subsistence of a slave or peasant. Or even the intolerance and ignorance that manifest in so many societies just several ages earlier and was little changed from thousands of cohorts earlier. Nor could those lucky folks truly conceive of the depravity and wanton poverty that beset so many other human beings across Earth, even while they lived in relative luxury, the hallmark being "might makes right."

This gives you an idea for your essay, having been reminded of the basic things for which you have to be grateful. You think about your Analysis class, which developed your critical thinking and helped you determine how best to lump, split, or otherwise draw parallels and divergences from what you see. You are adept at distilling away subterfuge, exposing the facts for what they are, then determining what they can tell you about the past, the future, and now.

Of course not everyone excels in Analysis as you do. You were told that you are one of great and infrequent talent; of that you are not really sure, it being irrelevant one way or the other. You might study Analysis further, as an academic discipline itself, but it is unlikely that you will consider it as a career, regarding it as a tool, with much mental masturbation after that.

And so, as you had learned to do in school, you think about humanity now versus before the Plague; comparing what is present now versus then, that being as good a partition as any. Countless tomes have been written, in many volumes, elaborating on this topic by scholars, this not being a new area of study. Fortunately for you in this circumstance, you haven't actually taken the time to read any of them. You start to make notes on the DCD and intend to refer to those made at the time of your Museum visit, when indicated; there were some phenomenal quotes as you recall. You're beginning to get excited. You'll start with the generalizations.

There is no hunger, no starvation; there are no wars; people are generally healthy. No insurance is needed. There certainly is no slavery. No one is exploited by any other person. There is no nationalism. There is no racism. There is no crime, no need for lawyers or police. There is peace on Earth.

When irreconcilable controversies occur, any citizen can argue his case as desired before a court of arbitration that changes daily and is staffed by citizens over a certain age; you're not sure just how old one has to be, but you know your parents are not yet eligible for such tribunals. These panels are always objective, making this means of settling disputes used only very rarely. Often the participants will feel sheepish afterwards when queried by their peers why they had to result to such depths to resolve a conflict.

There is a cornucopia of resources, or at least anything that anyone might need or want for their daily existence. Some things are technologically limited, being available for research purposes, but everyone, including those vying for the same, is understanding of this. Everyone is reasonable, even under these circumstances, knowing that they will be given the opportunity to test out their theories at some point, even if not immediately and they will certainly be able to find something else to do in the interim.

With long life, virtually no sickness, and effectively limitless natural resources providing all the power ever needed; no pollution of Wind and Water pure, where is the drama in life, your ancient ancestors might wonder? Where are the challenges? The conflict? Mankind would appear to have achieved true nirvana after the Plague, they would think. How would this peace on Earth operate on a daily basis?

You consider your desire to become a photographer and your earlier reflection that this was tentatively planned as your first vocation. Like many situations in life, career numbers in the individual instance fall under a general bell curve, with the mean somewhere around five to ten; some people have many more, with each lasting however long they desire; five to fifteen Rotations is typical. You learn and do what you want, whenever you want. What could be better than that, you wonder, this Analysis taking nothing for granted?

Like all students, you spend as much time in the fields, working the land and orchards, as you do in the classroom where you learn about art and literature, science and mathematics, philosophy and history. Most students spend fifteen to twenty Rotations learning basic skills and fundamental knowledge while growing food for Society. Your family moved to one of the farms, where the schools are also kept, after you were born, and you lived on several during your childhood. There are those naturally who spend the better parts of their lives on the farms. These elder farmers are not ridiculed or derided; quite the contrary, they are highly respected for their knowledge and insight, their patience and steadfastness, content in their daily endeavors. Nor are they celebrated with a wink, as if the bar of life had been lowered for them; that they choose to spend much of their lives in agriculture reflects their interests alone, certainly not their abilities.

Those with illustrious careers, who make many breakthroughs and create many original ideas are no more celebrated or revered than anyone else in the world. Nor are the great organizers or the artists; their notoriety gives them no special privileges. What could they need or want that they don't already have and which is not available to any other member of Society?

As your grandmother constantly reminds you, there is always someone better looking, smarter, or more capable at a particular task or problem; perhaps serendipity plays a role, with that person up to bat at a time of many converging factors. Regardless, but accordingly, there is no enmity for anyone's successes or adventures. Your plate is served from the same well stocked kitchen with the same portions. You choose what you want to attack and digest; you are respected as much as someone with much greater accomplishments.

It is a given, that while everyone has some basic intelligence, there being no mental deficiencies, hardly everyone is an intellectual. Still everyone is literate and reads. In fact, intelligence has remained under a general bell curve as well, with just a shift to the right. Like everyone else, you plan to work on and study those things you find interesting; the challenge lies within yourself to be content with your daily routine and your accomplishments. For in your satisfaction, lays Society's fulfillment.

There are really no rules per se. No one would ever want to encroach upon anyone else or their property and people try to do that which they have agreed to do. Nobody has anything that you can't have; if not now, then certainly at some reasonable point in your life. Thus, there is no purpose in taking something that doesn't belong to you.

You have another sip of your drink and empty the glass. You get up for more, from the kitchen. You've begun to lose track of the time. The DCD screen changes; your father is calling. He'll be home in an hour and a half, he says, just prior to the Interview. As you go from one room to another, the adjacent DCD keeps up with you so you can talk with complete freedom of movement, without losing your place or disrupting a conversation; that is how you have asked the system to respond for you. There are other options if you don't want to be shadowed; your mother can't stand this except during conversations with her parents.

You set your drink on the table and collapse back on the couch. Ah, you think, this feels good. For a few moments you rub your spine, head, and bottom into the cushions. You get a cashmere blanket from the other end, where you had left it yesterday, and place it over your shoulders. Now you feel better. You need to get back to work. On the DCD you review your thoughts. So far, you have the generalizations. Now to the specifics. You consider an expression you learned at the Museum: schwelds-r. While not in any order of significance, seriousness, or importance, each letter stands for a distinct difference in your Society versus that prior to the Plague. You won't leave anything out following this paradigm.

The first "s" is for stuff.

So if anything is available to all members of Society, what in fact does this 'anything' include? What doesn't it include, is the better question? Certainly covered are housing, food, furniture, clothing, appliances, vehicles and other transportation, diversions, work, art, knickknacks, and jewelry of course.

There isn't any need for money, credits or accounts of any type. For the first time in the history of Mankind, since the relative rareness and obdurate nature of gold was first noted, it ceased to have any value other than as a commodity; same thing for precious stones which had always been in great abundance, their price having been manipulated by powerful cartels.

Thus trifles that anyone wants are readily available, all

natural; there is no need for synthetics. Some people enjoy adorning themselves and own many different types that bring them pleasure; others find these of no particular significance or utility but don't begrudge those who do. On your desk is a one pound gold brick, a souvenir from one of your school trips to a mining camp; it is so soft, you have to be careful not to scratch or chip it. You visualize your mother's jewelry; she really isn't into that kind of stuff, you think, but she does have a flawless ten carat deep canary yellow diamond, pear shaped, a gift from your father upon your conception.

Consumer nonperishables such as clothing or appliances are recycled however often one desires.

All houses have the same basics. The average size is around 6000 square feet, with a plethora of rooms that can be readily redesigned as desired, copious space for offices, libraries, meditation, listening to music and other general entertainment, guests, saunas, whirlpools, swimming pools, as modern or traditional as desired. Some are much larger, mansions by any measure, and there are also some as small as one room cabins. Storage is generally plentiful, but isn't really needed since most items once no longer desired are simply recycled into their basic raw materials and reused. It is an efficient system, with much of housing and most other manufacturing being modular in design in one fashion or another. If you find a community that you like, but there is no home that suits you, you can have one torn down and another rebuilt; there are always people available and desirous of helping you since that is what they do. The diversity of people ensures that populations are widely distributed over Earth, most people living in a number of different communities at one time or another. There is still a bias towards cities, particularly with regard to manufacturing and work; but smaller towns and even rural areas thrive with those who choose that lifestyle. There are hermits; there are those who cannot bear to be alone, except in the bathroom.

Such abundance is possible because of the overall population, in the many billions; further there is a reasonable distribution at any given time of people wanting to do just about anything that needs to be done. Rarely is there a shortage of people for one task or another; every job save those at the higher levels of Organization, can accommodate as many workers as want to spend their days in that line of pursuit. Sometimes related to sudden swells of interest, there are temporary bottlenecks, but these are atypical because of the hoards of raw materials at all levels of life other than those currently under investigation in a research context, as noted.

While obvious technologic advances contribute substantially to the abundance of overall resources, no less a factor to be sure are the monumental savings. No longer are these flushed into the antique sewers that at one time brimmed with defense and war paraphernalia, financial services, insurance, crime and punishment, wasteful government, and much of the health care industry. There is still government, obviously; witness Minister Esse. She and thousands of others work tirelessly at their jobs, helping to keep the cogs of commerce, industry, and research reasonably balanced; it is no small task.

Whenever something material is desired, you look at possible options; there are usually multiple examples available. The differences are generally self evident, overkill in the one extreme, spartan at the other. If you can't find what you are looking for among generally manufactured goods, you contact the custom producers who are always available to accommodate you if possible, since that is what they do, custom work. Much shopping can be done from home, but there continue to be retail and shopping pavilions, the Markets (business and industry have their own Markets). There, representatives work whose only vested interest is helping you. Hosts and hostesses, not clerks or sales people, welcome you and help you find what you are seeking. They enjoy seeing the new merchandise and assisting others shop; these aren't drones, brainwashed on any physical or stimulus dependent Drug, repressed in one manner or another. Their previous or subsequent positions might include any level of esoterica, original thought, or Organization. Which portends one of the most intriguing features of your Society: if you don't know who you're dealing with, you should never underestimate a stranger. This sounds sinister, but menace cannot thrive where everyone is respected without reservation and is helped in any fashion by any other Citizen.

Sometimes at the Markets you enjoy the experience of simply looking around to see what's out there. Of course, you take whatever it is you want, or find that you didn't know you needed, or arrange to have it delivered to your home. The delivery people will notify you of their approximate time of arrival for courtesy, or they will let themselves in the door if you aren't home. No one locks their doors. Your privacy is assured since no one would ever snoop, and your possessions, if admired for the collection you have chosen to decorate your home, would never be filched for any reason. What possible rationale would one have for taking something enjoyed by someone else? This is how you grew up, like many generations of humans since the Plague.

Art, collectibles and genuinely unique artifacts constitute public treasures. Long ago the museums of Earth swapped their holdings, with entire exhibits and inventories of artists returned to the lands of their origins. The museums are open at all hours, all days; and works can be borrowed by individuals from time to time. The Manet in front of your stairs is the original. Virtually nothing is off limits, there being no problem in preservation and transport. Those minutiae are of no consequence; transportation is little more than hours from any one place on Earth to another. You can readily visit any museum or other locale in a day trip; hence your ability to go to and from Geneva today, traveling over 6000 miles each way. In fact your school has an upcoming excursion to Angkor Wat later this month; it will be a long day, you surmise, but an entertaining and educational one.

You're getting side tracked. The "w" in schwelds-r is for work.

So what kind of work is done? The kind of work that has always been done by women and men. Collecting and processing raw materials, manufacturing goods, providing services, research and development.

People are needed to run the machines; even though machines do much of the harder labor, they still require at least some guidance and maintenance. You recall the time in mining class you commanded the robotic processor to mine the silver in a certain side of a mountain and isolate the silver into 0.9999 pure product, reassembling the mountain as it went. No problems were encountered, but the thing still needed supervision. You had been chided by the instructor because while the machine could do what you asked, and did, it wasn't designed for that intensity. You had forced the processor to decide what specific tools would be utilized in the mining process, rather than making those decisions yourself, based on the terrain and other relevant details.

Some people like to work with their hands; their pleasure comes from manually imitating what machines could otherwise do, not just in Art, but also in basic assembly work. They often do custom jobs, which is desired about ten percent of the time in just about everything. Technology can provide with a much greater ratio if needed, but that number has been constant for hundreds of Rotations.

Computer aided Analysis of science and engineering makes possible designs that Mankind may never have noted or even considered. Nothing new here. Even before the Plague, Mankind already had sophisticated machines build ever more complex machines. But he was still assembling the prototypes. And his descendents still are. As complex as any machine has yet become, it's primary mission above all else is to guard and maintain human life, no exceptions. It doesn't mean an errant machine would be disassembled, but it would certainly undergo Analysis. These are very rare; you've read about them, but never seen one.

Any business is allowed to continue ad infinitum. At

one extreme there are those that are eminently successful and employ hundreds of thousands of workers from many different generations over hundreds of Rotations; at the other are those that produce nothing that any human needs or wants anymore, assuming they ever did. The only value they provide is their service to the Organizer, the sole remaining employee. In businesses without significant customers or clients, it is concluded by Society that you are studying the entity more than running it as a business, but that's ok too if that's how you choose to spend your time.

As tastes and customs change, so do styles. Workers shift with technologies, which are always developing, growing, or stagnating, or being discarded all together. At the more mundane level, when business gets to be so low that it is obvious the public is no longer interested in what you had to offer, either goods or services, you are happy to move on. The foreclosure is actually celebrated because so many people worked so hard for so many years, and earned great satisfaction through their professional affiliations with the establishment. There are many things that you planned on doing at some point, possibly in a tangent or something entirely different. Maybe you'll spend a few Rotations in Diversions.

Education and academics run the same gamut as they always have, but with a markedly positive shift. Everyone has the same basic education; some never have any more formally, but these are very rare. Nearly every job or career that you might seek will require some sort of training or apprenticeship, some lasting many Rotations, others months. You see what options are available and join the crew of your choice; their members are then responsible for you with the practical and specialized training that might be required, even if this means prolonged Rotations in specialty schools. A one Rotation commitment is recommended, but nothing is irrevocable; neither are starting and stopping dates. But work isn't a game of musical chairs. Further prolonged didactic training culminating in advanced degrees, "the smaller twin conjoined to research and development," a phrase you picked up from the

Museum, usually requires enough Rotations that the recipients may look upon that education as an experience unto itself. Most people embrace their future work, both practical and less so. You can always return to formal education and earn advanced degrees, even after many previous jobs and endeavors. There are still "egg heads with their hands figuratively traversing the elastic band of their undergarments, going whoopee over solving a puzzle, the tension crescendoing!" Another expression. Some people are students for much of their lives, going from one discipline to another, never at the research level, learning a little bit about just about every topic on Earth. While quirky to say the least, they are substantially older than most of the scholars who teach and certainly the bulk of the students; nevertheless, they are highly respected given their learning and perseverance; their input is always enjoyed and encouraged. There is everything in between the life time student and the fanatics. Admittedly scholars are plentiful; but what would you rather have, armies of scholars or armies of soldiers?

Some lessons of the pre-Plague era are still with humanity. The art of war remains practiced, as a game yes, but also as training. Most people participate at one time or another in these exercises, several Rotations, during which they become experts in weapons use as a means of destroying specific targets. Resource diversion to armaments is miniscule, not worth a second lick of the spoon, and the emphasis is on defense of Earth from a hostile Alien Species, with appropriate counter measures. The games are highly realistic in terms of other Species having more advanced weapons, but not necessarily insurmountable; while great fun and an honor to participate, they are felt to be more of a sport rather than strategic training. Because of Mankind's circumspection on other worlds, no conflict has ever required military input in any fashion. So people play, you mean train; you won't be eligible for these civic duties for another fifty Rotations. You wonder if the Aliens' visit will mean harm, or if possibly they want to relocate all humans or worse yet, exterminate Mankind entirely, with the warning to get out now or don't bother, everything in this sector will be demolished?

On a more optimistic note, you consider the impact of the unfolding events on the news. While probably occupying ever larger parts of human news stories hereafter, there will continue to be disharmony, personal opinions, preferences, and cliques. Universal agreement hardly exists, but now most everyone is reasonable when speaking their mind. Regardless of the topic, words are never antagonizingly blunt with the purpose of hurting feelings, but more to portend various options, the advice is offered without agenda and freely able to be discarded without malice. Nor is conversation innuendo by another name. No one is around to irrevocably change your mind with regard to anything, which helps you grow up pretty fast once you are no longer a child on one of the farms. No one is around to harm you and you can ask anyone for assistance with a problem and they will see to it that help arrives promptly. You may freely communicate with anyone on Earth and in Space, as desired.

You know that even now, well maybe not right now, you could contact Minister Esse, and she would personally speak with you in private. Nevertheless, pandemonium is not present because you would never embarrass yourself by contacting someone at a certain level unless you were sure you could make a positive contribution, even with constructive criticism. Most everyone, regardless of their work or position in Society, specifically makes time for speaking with individuals about various questions or concerns they might have, enjoying the sharing of their knowledge, hoping to inspire someone into their current field of inquiry or work. From these regular sessions, it has been found that great insight can be garnered by presentation of the simplest of questions. You won't be eligible to be on the giving side of this equation for at least eighty Rotations, possibly less depending on how your studies and productivity evolve; timing is really irrelevant anyways and there are always exceptions.

The news still shows people and their actions, but now

it is about their positive events that people find interesting, rather than the evil acts that brought them to infamy. You shudder at the thought of reading about all the crime and heartache that punctuated so much of pre-Plague life; you wonder if they were making all that up, whoever the they is. The news is a means of discussion as well as highlighting areas of trend, local, regional, state, national, Global or Stellar, all within the context of Minister Esse's approbation. Because each reporter or journalist has such a diverse background, it makes for news as accurate as can be reported, and without hyperbole or propaganda. Most adults eat this up, but until recently you found the news and current events relatively boring, despite the fact that your teachers attempted to draw parallels from your daily studies. It's a kid thing, you think.

The "d" in schwelds-r is for diversions.

While in school, much of your time is spent in diversions. On the Farms there are hundreds or thousands like you in each community, depending on the size and type of the harvest assembled. There are occasional children raised and educated in the mining camps. There is no reason for this not to be more prevalent, their environment is as pastoral and bucolic as any agricultural setting; it just doesn't work out that way. Maybe you'll investigate this further some day, you think. As you have matured, the distinction between diversion and work has become a fine one; any work done by you brings contentment and is productive in one fashion or another, or you won't continue it long; but diversion also affords great satisfaction that is not clearly productive beyond providing you with satisfaction if you look to a relatively broad definition. Millions of people work in the entertainment industry; define entertainment as any play, anything not specifically designed to produce anything but contentment on the part of the player. There are games of all types with real or surrogate partners: board games, mind games, some abstract, some based on historical conditions, electronic and computer games, meditation, recreational Drugs, vacations and sightseeing, gambling, music, literature, theatrical productions, dance, stories visually recreated or read by electronic media or other. There continue to be sports of all types and levels, but women never compete with men, since it just wouldn't be fair.

The "l" in schwelds-r is for love. While love and sex could be pigeonholed under diversions or health, these emotions and behaviors are so distinctly different from pre-Plague existence that they warrant a separate letter.

Sex remains a major diversion, of course to many, to be practiced toward whatever ritualization by whatever means you and your spouse find mutually satisfying. But other than the physical act of "creaming the pie," you see in your Museum notes, sex in your Society bears no resemblance to the acts of lust, procreation, or the dirty detritus that yoked pre-Plague men. There is a marked contrast to the random fucking that caused so much despair prior to the Plague; not despair but "War, murder, mayhem, torture, robbery, slavery, prostitution, suicide, madness, incest, child molestation, pornography," referring again to your notes from the Museum.

While you've read about the evolution of love and sex in the married couple and you are now dating, your recently married Analysis teacher keeps you apprised of the spirit, if not details, of human sexuality. She and her husband were married about six months ago, having dated exclusively for two Rotations. They were engaged in the early part of the last Rotation, which would be a reasonable focal point to conclude that they were in love, whatever that meant, other than the obvious connotation that they planned to be married in the near future and proclaim their love before God and all Society. So in this context the advent of love cannot be observed until it is complete, although there are no doubt telltale signs along the way to any but the most doltish observer of the participants. You can remain in love and never get married but the relationship will be forever handicapped, you recall learning.

Love is a gradual process, you surmise. You will know when you are there and have found it, but not necessarily before, and probably as the result of a culmination of factors both major and minor in terms of compatibility. No doubt one person of the couple experiences this emotion before the other one, at least by some period. Again this is just guesswork on your part; you certainly aren't old enough to fall in love. While there are no definitive rules prescribing the length of courtship or age of marriage, statistics have shown that most people date their future mate for at least a couple Rotations and generally don't wed until they are well past thirty Rotations old.

You think back to your teacher's union of a half Rotation and their dating for some time before that. From what she has intimated, and her situation so far is on schedule by your mental arithmetic, she and her husband have yet to engage in sexual intercourse and achieve a climax. They cuddle together every night, your teacher effusing how good her lover feels in her arms. You imagine your future husband doing the same, wondering about the warmth and exhilarating tingles that will fire through your body. Of this you have no personal experience at this point in your very young life. You do know they kiss and fondle each other, since you already do the same with the occasional young men that you find sufficiently stimulating and special. And you suspect that they also explore each other down intimate oral avenues, a behavior that you can't even fathom although you have read that it is exquisitely pleasurable. Oh...my...God, you had thought, when you first learned about this in school.

So when will they start screwing or achieving an orgasm other than through coitus? How long do people have to be married before "sex" can occur? There is no absolute answer to this question you know, but studies have shown a relatively even distribution, centering around one Rotation—after marriage of course. There are always a few, coming in well beyond any reasonable number of standard deviations; it has always been rumored, an old wives' tale so to speak, that consummating the marriage either exceptionally late or statistically very early augurs for dynamically sensuous love making when this ability kicks in. You recall reading this even before you were a teenager, though you now know this has never been verified, and think that may have been a book of fiction. How funny, you think, your mind wandering again to the pre-Plague existence of your Species. So much wasted energy, time, and attention; women, and curiously men in particular, spent "mentally fucking or at least sexually assessing a member of the opposite sex that they encountered throughout their daily routines, obviously only one of whom was their spouse, assuming they were even married at all! And daily routines had to be defined very broadly, so as to include pornography as well as the five level hierarchy of womanhood**, not to mention the diversions that spawned rape and incest! Incredibly, the overwhelming majority of men were monoplanar, being summed up best by the two word question, each thought dominating one side of their brain, Got... beaver?" You refer to your notes again.

What the fuck? you think. (Your parents don't give a shit whether you cuss [DJS: in an imperfect Society, where disappointment still occurs, there will be disenchantment, which can only be translated into Ancient English as cussing], as long as you do it under the right circumstance; which is not around anyone who would find it offensive and certainly not around young children. Your parents know they are only words, but some people are just more sensitive. As far as children are concerned, they will learn these soon enough when they go to school, even if they don't encounter this vocabulary at home.)

But back to your disbelief. You've had several boyfriends including your current beau; you are not a child after all. Your experience with each of them has been so different, the way they kiss and fondle your body through your clothing; some with gentle caresses, others with paws that help delineate a different masher. Still, each provides you with varying stimulation. The receptors in your skin, your oral mucosa, your tongue and nose, ingeniously designed biologic transducers, convert perception of light touches, pressure, movement, warmth, aroma, and taste into electrical impulses that shower the brain with enlightenment in ways that vision and hearing leave lacking. Which is not to minimize the eroticism that optical and auditory data can and do provide you in your exploration of your sensuality.

In school you had sex education as part of your study of human anatomy and physiology, required subjects in your earlier classroom years. You quite understand the "birds and the bees;" a quaint expression you recall from the Museum. You are anxious to learn more at the personal level, which can only come about from physical intimacy. Of course it is not required for satisfaction in your relationships, let alone places them in jeopardy. Yet, emotional and sensory interchanges with another put into motion the love chemicals first synthesized in your body with the advent of puberty. With each encounter, your molecules are sparked by those provided by your partner, resulting in a crescendo in some relationships, followed by gradual decay as it becomes clear that your friendship will go no further; but each time to a higher static level, rarely lower. Ultimately a threshold is reached, at least from what you have read and from what your teacher has discussed, whereby you realize you are in love with the other person and make plans to be married. With the vows of marriage imprinted in your memory, further cascades of dendritic reshuffling will occur, ever more finely tuned to the specific counterparts with which your husband endows you during periods of intimacy and vice versa. Eventually, with sufficient stimulation in this context, you and your lover will become one and begin experiencing sex, in all its divinations.

This final threshold, the ability to sexually climax, will only come about after marriage, after sufficient biological time, and will be unique to your spouse. This being the bottom line: no woman or man is physically capable of undertaking sexual intercourse and achieving an orgasm, either through coitus directly or from other stimulation, unless in love and married to one who loves as dearly, and with whom they have been intimate in this status on a regular basis for a substantial period of time. No amount of manual and oral persuasion, pharmaceuticals, or surgical alteration can induce a woman's vagina to accommodate any insertion, no man can achieve an erection and no one is capable of having an orgasm without sex having been kindled by the synergism of love and marriage.

You know that you and your husband will have little clear warning prior to that special night. After months of fondling and kissing, intercourse and orgasm become a natural extension of your play, prior to sleep. Thereafter, sex will become a regular and integral part of your lives, frequency and options to be determined by individual tastes; mutual contentment guaranteed. You have read that the subsequent pleasures can become a potent subset of the matrix that binds wife and husband; but you have also read that sex will always remain just that, an ingredient of the glue, not a panacea that resets the circuits of people in a mindless, robotic construct.

In contradistinction to pre-Plague Mankind, you and your husband will have no carnal interest in any person other than your spouse. Hence, sex outside of marriage and love, in all its potentially fiendish permutations is simply not possible. While you realize that porn could be made by a willing couple, no one other than themselves would find it of any erotic value. Although your society places no taboos against nudity, overall modesty remains the general persuasion. For those who truly eschew clothing or portions thereof, they typically practice such costumes in private, knowing that they wouldn't get any deleterious or positive feelings from others.

Where there is love and marriage there is also divorce, at least in your Society; while most couples do, mating for life is not required. But divorce is nothing like that which shattered so many lives in millennia long past. The dissolution of marriage is no longer shunned as it was by most societies at one time or another, "making hypocrites out of the bulk of the adult population, assuredly more male than female," you recall from the Museum tour. You also remember reading about periods when the rubber band of temperance was stretched taut, with huge portions of the population racked by the discontinuity of fractured marriages. Divorce now remains well described, but rare indeed; always resulting from partners growing apart, almost never related to physical incompatibility. As interest in their spouse begins to wane, sex is the first to go in a relationship. Under these circumstances, your love chemicals begin to diverge from your loved one's, but this etching down is generally very gradual and step wise, no geometric algorithms at play here. Parting is always cordial. Both participants are a bit sad, but each is understanding of this lack of accord and interested in their and their previous spouse's ultimate well being. Without appropriate, ongoing stimulation, neither divorced party will be having sex again for quite some number of Rotations. They can and most do fall in love again, after sufficient time, but they can expect a courtship at least twice as long as previously experienced. Still, as infrequent as divorce is nowadays, those so disposed by fate have experiences that few others do. That doesn't give them notoriety in any fashion and, not surprisingly, no one really gives a shit as long as they are happy.

Now you have further read that there are many whose lives do not fall into this "heteronormative status quo," this seemingly being inconsistent with the need for certain factors for growth and development that are required as one ages, biologically ensuring that almost everyone has a loving life partner. Their marriages are as blessed as anyone else's. The obvious affection and care that they share for one another, both female-female and male-male, being such that their bodies are able to adapt accordingly. As it has always been since the beginning of Mankind, some prefer their own sexually to the opposite sex; the numbers are relatively small, but in contrast to ancient times, now like with everything else, nobody gives a shit one way or the other as long as you are content. "Ancient bigots be damned, nonheterosexual couples never did, are not currently, and never will bring down the populace!" you quote again. Not that you've ever known one.

The "c" in schwelds-r is for children.

So where do children come from in this State of Cornucopia, with a working equilibrium between jobs, people, technology, education; in a population of many billions no less? Reports from other Worlds bring the no longer surprising finding that there are millions of the buggers about. Thinking of all that fucking you just described would perhaps suggest that large percentages of children are born on Earth as well, making it possible for anyone who wanted to have a child to do so. This is exactly what happens, sort of, which means qualitatively if not quantitatively. Only to those couples whose love and overall nature and compatibility, tolerance, and understanding both individually and collectively, coming together at an appropriate time in the couple's marriage, is a child conceived and born. The birth rate is very rare, making children truly gifts from Above, given to those special couples who will be most adept at raising the next generation. Overall, the birth rate is ever so slightly greater than the mortality statistics, but these have changed only fractions of percents in many hundreds of Rotations.

You return your empty glass to the kitchen. You stretch, raising your arms above your head and tensing the muscles in your legs. You do this several times, followed by some deep, controlled breathing. You look outside. Thc luster of the Sun and the breeze you see sifting the crops beckon you. You're making progress on the essay, but you would love some outside air and the massage of those photons on your skin. You decide to put on your sunflower bathing suit and go out on the patio and work. You still have an hour or so before the Conference. While upstairs in your bedroom, you look at yourself in the full length mirror after removing your gray pin striped suit and underwear. Your tan lines are so distinct, you actually appear to be still wearing a bra and panties; you can't help smiling, thinking how your boyfriend really likes this. You go outside with your PCD, arrange yourself comfortably on one of the lounge chairs, and begin again.

The "h" in schwelds-r is for health.

Contemporary health and longevity are nothing like the diseases and unnecessary deaths of many Rotations gone by. Your health is generally excellent, requiring little maintenance, as is everyone else's. You have had various injuries, all minor, thank goodness; long bone fractures, abrasions, and at one point a minor concussion, all while undertaking gymnastic maneuvers that were too advanced for your level of skill. You had, of course, healed completely, with little overall alteration of your life style at the time, common sense being the key for a change. Although relatively speaking, you are not that much of a dare devil.

You can look forward to a very long life, barring the truly unforeseen. Even with severe injuries, as long as brain function can be maintained at a certain level, tissue regeneration is truly phenomenal. While the body is not indestructible by any means, cellular refurbishment occurs quite handsomely over several months; with excellent, if not perfect restoration possible with appropriate effort on the injured's part. Imagine the first people after the Plague who noted this obviously new found ability of Mankind, you ponder. Given the regenerative properties, which rarely need any outside augmentation by professionals, surgery is almost never required except in the most extreme situations, wherein "exogenous means of nutrition are required to fuel the subcellular explosion of organelles needed for the greatly amplified cellular turnover, angiogenesis, synaptic sprouting, cascades of immune responses and so on," you see in your notes. Of course if the brain is too significantly destroyed or the body as well, enough to affect the brain, then someone dies; this fortunately is very rare.

Aging has been markedly slowed in all cellular groups after about twenty Rotations; thus, cartilaginous joints and discs, muscle fibers, neurons, epithelial and all differenttiated cells are far more robust, able to reproduce and maintain themselves in excellent condition for virtually the life of the person. Moreover, no one can ever harm anyone else, consciously or unconsciously; this is hardwired into the brain in multiple redundant pathways. To destroy these pathways would end the life of the person. Accidents happen, as they always will, but again the brain factors probabilities of any action or inaction with regard to human life; and the industrial complex is such that machinery also has multiple means of assessing situations and their possible outcomes on a moment by moment basis. You simply cannot imagine what would have gone through someone's mind as they brutalized, maimed, murdered or tortured another human being, as you've read was the fashion in the pre-Plague era. Except through stupidity or lack of experience, you cannot direct any machine to undertake an action that would be harmful to someone else, and your supervisor would never allow you such freedom until you are fully prepared to handle the situation. This isn't as dire as it might sound since pushing your individual envelope is encouraged from childhood, just with appropriate and adequate backup. That's why your gymnastic injuries weren't more severe.

Physically you are competitive. You have exercised for as long as you can remember; all but a few people enjoy some challenge and regular deployment of their bodies. Currently you are playing on the school ji-dai team, a sport unknown during the earlier civilizations of Mankind, but one which invariably involves an object being propelled in one direction or another by the players, governed by certain rules. In this regard, the object and concept are always the same; you decide what kind of exercise you would like, over what time period, and what conventions best fit your temperament. The game can be physically exhausting over the ninety minutes of play, subject to reasonable time outs. Your team will play the Mid-Asian champions next week, at their home, the women's team, needless to say. Women never compete physically with men. Not allowed, since it would be a slaughter [DJS: a seemingly foreign concept in Eartherian that can only be translated thusly]. From basic science courses in school, you understand the reason, this being one of those explanations that requires molecular analysis, the body habitus is merely a façade. As in the pre-Plague era, men are far more muscular in appearance and fact than women, who continue to have delicate limbs and chests, long sculpted necks and facial features, tapered abdomens and waists, and hips generally one-third larger than their waists, plus or minus a few per cent. Thus the magic below the surface, in the very proteins of muscle contraction; those of women are structurally different from men's, with a morphology that is strikingly more efficient, gram for gram. Hence no man could ever physically take on a woman in any fashion and, naturally, no woman would want to beat the shit out of any man. What would she gain?

Menstruation now lasts a single day, bleeding is light and produces no cramps or alteration in one's psyche. Beginning at puberty, you can alter your appearance at will in terms of hair color and style and nails, these appendages responding within minutes of your decision to change as you become an adult; certainly, hair grows only where you want it. You run your index finger through your banana curls, as you lay your head back and close your eyes to the Sun's dazzle. They are coming along nicely, you think, recalling the image in your mirror. You have mentally been working on these for days, the brown luster iridescent, but the style only gradually taking shape, a sign of adolescence, much like skin eruptions in pre-Plague teens. Where applicable, these abilities apply to men as well; no longer must the majority attend to facial shaving to feel tidy. Both men's and women's voices change during the teen years, but boys' never squeak .

All of the above stand as positive functions in health and well being, post-Plague. What is no longer present? Huge lists can be distilled down to two words: no disease. You have read about ancient scourges, complete with pictures of the pathology, pre and post mortem; ugly cannot begin to describe your perception of birth defects, cancer, heart disease, stroke, arthritis and other auto-immune disorders, uremia, diabetes, hypertension, obesity, and any degeneration, or so called metabolic disorder. Ultimately, all disease is explained within the context of specific cellular machinery gone awry. Many millennia ago, this cellular dysfunction, perhaps a type of premature aging, would result from "the accumulation or deficiency of a specific subcellular protein or other factor, by one means or another, endogenously or exogenously instigated," you see in the window of your PCD containing the Museum notes.

There is no significant pain now, that being noted is to alert you to the possibility of a local malfunction, at the cellular level, which might prompt the appropriate health officials to augment your system with boosters or other medication. You have not required one of these and statistically you won't. When required, they work the overwhelming majority of the time, or at least that is your general understanding of medication. Your interaction with the field has been minimal and this has never been a great interest to you one way or the other.

Infectious disease remains, with environmental homeostasis requiring some evolution of bugs, but woe unto those that try to lunch on your body. Any infestation is readily smacked down with a fool proof system of redundant and cascading arrays that can gear up for any invasion, regardless of load and virulence. If necessary, your cells will go into hibernation, the DNA indestructible. The virus or other agent has no way of reproducing, thus dying off and discarded as other enzymes come into play while your DNA is sequestered. You rhetorically ask, could other agents be developed that can overcome these current defenses? Yes, of course, it is rare to find a lock without a key, even if one has to be custom made. But they would have to be intentionally designed, which would never be done by any human, and on an evolutionary basis, this is also possible, tens of thousands of Rotations hence, but you suspect Mankind's ability to deal with them will be appropriately enhanced by then.

You know you are not immortal, nothing is. Death is not welcomed, but when it comes, it is not feared and there is no regret. Death is foreshadowed by some slight infirmity in the older person, usually approaching 300

Rotations, if not older. This is the admonition to him or her that sometime in the next several months, they will probably pass away. Thus if there are any last plans or desires which have yet to be fulfilled, highly unlikely for most, then now is the time to do it; their long life has freed them up from any general impatience. Health is otherwise unchanged, with the individual being somewhat slow as they had been for many Rotations in terms of locomotion, but not acumen. Thus life is completed; one is laid to rest typically while asleep, dying like a rat (which is the greatest way to go and especially appealing for your lover) or with some really great Drugs.

Still, life is not perfect, you have read. There are circumstances, relatively infrequent in the extreme, wherein individuals become irreparably ill and pass away far sooner than normal for your Species. These are especially loved by their spouses, families, and communities in general; they are not martyrs and they do not suffer. Everyone understands that some things just can't be helped; the goal is to enjoy the time one has. Though most people can plan on a very long life indeed, these unfortunate souls are in everyone's thoughts and prayers and remind the community at large to be more thankful for the blessing of good health that the bulk of the population enjoys. Surviving spouses in these circumstances almost always fall in love again, but great time is required to settle one's thoughts, and your first spouse will forever be a part of your heart, intertwined into your very being.

There are no psychiatric problems, no disabling stress or depression, no psychoses. But there is without doubt silliness, forgetfulness, and inattention at times. People continue to be animated and appropriately despondent when indicated.

The Sun's luminescence bakes your skin. You are getting hot and have finished your drink. Droplets of perspiration are propelled down your cleavage, a few lodging in your belly button before returning to Wind. Time to go in, you think. Tan corduroy shorts with matching suspenders and a short sleeved knit shirt replace your two piece suit. Being outside was exhilarating. You sit on the Indian rug in your bedroom and the DCD takes over where you left off with your PCD. You review your essay, trying to think of anything else about health that you might have left out or want to include. This is tough, you conclude; you're stuck.

You think back to your conversation with Jizelle, about how registration was "fine." It was at some level, but the crushing rendition of your name and the need for the additional essay made this "not fine;" hence, at some level, you lied. There is a clear distinction between truth and fiction, of course, something that all young children learn. Nevertheless, lying is never done to harm anyone. In this enlightened Society, you wonder how it is possible for one to be able to lie. You suspect that this has been studied in detail although you have not investigated the explanation. Your internal rationale has concluded that without lies, there can be no imagination, since a lie is a postulate of sorts, a challenge to reality if for no other purpose than to act as a counterpoint.

The "r" in schwelds-r is for religion.

Religion still exists, above all during testing when you are not entirely prepared! But seriously, there are agnostics still, though they are the exception. Most everyone enjoys some spirituality with their Creator, there being numerous forms of worship and devotion, both as collectives and individually. Organized faith remains firmly entrenched, but there is no proselytizing. Forced conversions or intolerance are impossible.

The second "s" in schwelds-r is for species, other.

Nearly all humans have pets, particularly since children are so rare. You've had dogs and occasional cats and you're not even a real adult yet. Some people are partial to fish or birds; you like these well enough, but wouldn't want any as companions. Many birds are relatively domesticated, happy to stay in your yard and interact with you, doing tricks or resting nearby, singing tunes when asked, and sharing the joy of their offspring. Similarly, some fish don't mind living in relatively small environments. Some people have even more esoteric animals as pets, including reptiles, amphibians, and other mammals; the key is mutual tolerance; not all creatures are capable of living domestically with Mankind.

Bugs and other vermin are not pets. Unlike microbes, insects and other irritating life forms have restricted Wind, Water, and Earth space; they must at all times remain at least 150 feet from any human, adjusting their perimeter according to the movement of Mankind. This is accomplished by pheromones produced by people that are instantly toxic to such Species; though any person who is studying or helping said creatures can reduce the production of these chemical repellents. Still, no animal could ever irreparably harm a human; any hostile action immediately produces a lethal castoff of olfactory stimuli, rendering the predator harmless.

Animals remain fodder for one another, that being the way of Earth, survival of the fittest at some level; however, they are no longer on Mankind's menu, under any circumstances. Everyone is a strict vegetarian, "not out of some fringe counter cultural imbecilic guilt about consuming something produced by anything with a face (define face!)," you recall reading at the Museum. Rather, no meat or organic, nonvegetarian proteins or other compounds can be digested by humans. It's as simple as that; after the Plague, Mankind's teeth and digestive systems could no longer process such material and the taste became unpleasant, at least from what you have read about that time period. You certainly would never try to consume any flesh or other animal substrate! Human babies are nursed by their mothers, that being entirely different.

The last letter, the "e" in schwelds-r is for the Elements.

Wind and Water have achieved nirvana with Mankind and Earth, meaning that weather has been mastered. All are happy to exist in equilibrium. There are still periodic outbursts, yet never in a way that seriously threatens anything more than property, which can be replaced or repaired if it's of historical interest.

Your Analysis and the essay are almost complete as far as you are concerned, there being one last marked difference between the pre- and post-Plague periods: and that relates to fire [DJS: which no longer requires capitalization]. The nature of fire was finally determined, allowing it to be extinguished once and for all by instilling antifire elements throughout all manufactured and grown materials as well as the atmosphere. This took place about fifty Rotations before the weather was mollified; you will have to look this up later, making a note in the margin. There continues to be abundant heat and limitless energy, but never again would any living creature in either the animal or plant kingdoms be harmed by the flames of fire. The controversy over what to do with fire was fierce. Some felt it would be a shame never to feel the warmth of the flame in a wonderful hearth, for example, as they cuddle with their spouse. But overall it was concluded that since fire had wreaked such havoc over the millennia and made miserable so many people's lives, that it should be banished once and for all. Despite the fact that your body is no longer readily susceptible to combustion and fire really could be controlled, Mankind simply didn't want to bother with it anymore. When humans are away from Earth on other worlds, fire is typically encountered; those flames immediately recognize that humans have fire's answer (antidote) and are not to be trifled with so they are never burned when away from Earth either, even if openly confronted. This is often to the chagrin of the Locals, so confrontations with fire are avoided now, everywhere.

You finish the essay at this point, knowing you will need to proofread it later and do some editing; you will also contemplate possible conclusions from consideration of the data. The DCD screen in your bedroom returns to the default. You will also want your parents' reviews, before sending it to the Registrar. You have plenty of time. It is now just a few minutes before the Conference.

As you walk downstairs, your parents come home simultaneously, just in time. Your mother is back from orbit and has lots of packages; she is bubbling. Your father is also quite excited; his work for the last twenty Rotations has been centered on stellar charts and gravimetric fields, attempting to postulate the location of star systems with planets that might foster other sentient life forms.

You exchange greetings, hugs, and kisses and have a seat in the living room. You start to ask about their day and the contents of the packages, when the DCD screen flashes three red lights again for a few moments, the sound returns, and Minister Esse and an Alien are broadcast around the Globe. You can see them! They have not actually begun speaking yet. Surely, everyone in the world, short of someone involved in a dying dead dog fit, is watching. This is the most momentous day in eons, indeed the most exciting day in your life, and you're not even directly involved.

# Book 8 Minister II

SINCE THE WEATHER had been mastered, long before even your grandparents were born, Mankind has rarely interfered other than with appropriate nudges. You learned about this traditional Ministerial policy in school and continue it currently, anticipating that all who succeed you will do the same. Thus your meteorologists direct adequate amounts of Water for production of any type of crop, anywhere it is desired to be grown. Other than this, Wind, Water, and Earth are free to have reasonable commotion at will, up to but not including devastation. Still, there are very infrequent exceptions to this plan of non-interference and today certainly constitutes one.

Accordingly, throughout Earth, the weather is calm; there is no precipitation and cool breezes comfort where appropriate. You and one of the Aliens sit at a table in the Council Center, across from your residence. The room is heptagonal in design, each side representing one continent of Earth; tables interlock bounded on the outside by high, open backed chairs made of dark brown, soothing cushions. At the center of the room, a huge DCD is mounted, the three dimensional display for all to see. From the ceilings, which are about thirty feet tall, emanates the lighting, like all modern structures, the brightness, color intensity, and direction of accentuation adjustable, as desired for the occasion. Today the lighting is pleasingly bright, but soft; there are no spotlights. The walls and floor are tiled, with progressive hues of the visible spectrum, from violet to red covering the former, the colors shifting every hour; the floor consists of a mosaic of the star systems in which Mankind has found sentient life forms, remaining a work in progress.

After you and your husband were contacted last night, you instantly changed your red curls to a simple but elegant chignon and put on one of your favorite dresses, a mid-calf, creamy outfit of linen. It has a fitted waist, a walking vent, short sleeves that don't cover your shoulders, and black trim surrounding the mandarin collar; moreover, it is lined so you don't have to wear a slip. The only jewelry you decided to wear, besides your wedding band of course, is your flat platinum necklace that holds an eight carat marquis cut black diamond, a gift from your parents when you became Minister.

You, your Chancellor and Vice-Minister have been speaking with three of the Aliens since last night. You are communicating in your native tongue, Eartherian, which they apparently know quite well. Clearly they have done their homework. The broadcast begins. Which means you begin. After all, you are the big cheese.

"All Eartherians, behold and welcome to our home, the Peregrinians. Let me assure you first that they come in Peace. They have the technology to bypass all of our settlements and observation outposts; they were not detected until they landed, not far from here actually. I have had the opportunity to speak with them about their purpose here, but please understand I am not any more privy to their design than you are. We have exchanged pleasantries and I understand their home is about five hours from Earth, at only one-half ISD speed, no less. We've been neighbors all these thousands of Rotations, but never met. That was their doing, much to our vexation; they apparently know us quite well, even as we know them not at all. Their representative, Ambassador Adavan, asked that I introduce them to Eartherians in this format and allow them to clarify through our discussion today, this momentous day I might add, questions that I am sure are on everyone's mind. Ambassador?"

Your gaze is fixed on the Peregrinian Ambassador Adavan. Your ears surround each of his words, not allowing a single syllable to escape your complete assessment. As a race they stand erect and are anthropomorphic, insofar as they have a bilaterally symmetric head and face, torso, and multiple appendages. But then, you think, by that definition, they could be giant bugs, which they certainly are not; if for no other reason than they don't have antennae and they do have an endoskeleton. The Ambassador is about six feet tall, although one of the others was much shorter and the other taller still; they said there is a great variety in terms of their height and other features, depending on their genealogy. They locomote on two appendages with very small feet and wear no shoes; on the bottoms of their feet are hardened circumferential cushions of tissue that actually make contact with the ground. From what they said, they are extremely resilient in terms of abrasions, which accounts for them not having to wear artificial protective coverings; moreover, they have increased agility over uneven terrain. Their torso consists of broad shoulders and chest, barrel shaped, which tapers into what would have to be an abdomen that is flattened and only about a third the diameter of their upper body. What appears to be hair covers their entire bodies, including their faces, at least what you can see. Copper colored, soft appearing garments with a neck line plunging about three inches below the center in a tight triangle and short sleeves cover their body, stopping just below the start of their legs; it appears to be one piece. Adavan's neck is short, whereas other Peregrinians can have long ones. Their heads are large with sunken eyes, an ear on each side; their bony skull extends forward making a projected hard palate with a movable jaw on the bottom, their teeth like humans designed for eating vegetation. There are both upper and lower teeth and a nose at the end, dark and glistening. Their nostrils flare at times, particularly when they sigh. Larger and coarser hairs adorn each side of their faces, just behind their noses. Their upper extremities, two, are highly flexible, their joints allowing virtually free movement; at the ends are tough cushions, like on their feet; their dexterity with these is incredible as they demonstrated in a game of concentration and coordination last night. Finally, they have a fifth appendage, extending from below their waist, in the back, projecting from their clothing; you think, a tail? No, you'll have to ask Adavan what they call this; you see it moves freely in the air, and one of them last night said something about increased balance and maneuverability. Their heads bob, but only when they speak. From what they have told you, individually they are as unique, both cognitively and physically as humans are. Their lineage also dictates the length of their hair, the curliness, fineness, and colors of this integument protection; the shape, size, length, and angle of projection of their ears and fifth appendages. They said it is customary for each Peregrinian to wear a ring of metal or synthetic polymer around their necks, loosely fit; upon these rings fits a medallion that also has free movement in this plane, adorned with their names and the coordinates of their homes. One of Adavan's assistants said last night that she was female; to your human eyes there was little difference between her and the others, although you have to admit, having only seen the three, she did appear to be less muscular and more delicate than the other two. She said that she has had twenty children and showed you their pictures; not all at once, of course. Of course, you had responded.

"We, of Peregrine, salute your Species and look forward to a long and mutually favorable relationship with Earth. As you were just informed, we are here on a Peaceful endeavor. There is no conquest. You have no need for any defensive posture. No one will be harmed in any fashion or have their lives disrupted in any manner. That is not our purpose here. We do not desire anything from you other than the Truth and recognition thereof when it is presented. This might sound ominous, but I assure you there are no sinister designs and our only method of engagement is gentle conversation.

"But before I explain more, particularly concerning the timing of our visit to your serene World, Minister Esse, and all who are listening, let me answer the questions that I know are, if not at the forefront of your thoughts, not far from there.

"You want to know 'How long have we possessed ISDs? How could you have missed seeing us before now? Are there other Species with ISDs, from other worlds, you haven't encountered?'

"You want to know 'Do we have advanced technology?'" He pauses and smiles, his eyes widening; his fifth appendage curls upward and moves back and forth. "Does a hobby horse have a hickory dick? Your language is so colorful! And your ongoing hubris is one of the things we like about your Species. Let's see. Our weapons, which we haven't used, but continue to update with ongoing practices, were developed in conjunction with our ISDs, somewhat before your Species developed the simple bow! Now I wonder... We have traveled Space for quite some time you see and in the Consortium to which we belong, we are only middle-aged in terms of evolution. Hence, just because you never observed other Worlds that had developed ISDs, didn't mean they weren't out there. We have watched over you in Space since your first ISD testing; and came to your aid, protecting your ancestors at times from incipient disasters. As you well know, your interstellar history has documented phenomena and statistical failures that inexplicably didn't result in complete devastations. There were occasional deaths that even we couldn't avoid. Rest assured, we are not gods and make no claim over life and death after a certain point in any Species.

"Now I would like to place this visit in historical context.

"We have watched Earth for many tens of thousands of Rotations, with much greater attentiveness in the last 7000 or so; with few exceptions, most everyone we knew viewed Mankind as a fucking [DJS: once again, this is the best English translation from Eartherian] joke. We knew some kind of Armageddon was coming; we just weren't sure in what fashion your Species would choose to go and what would be the aftermath. Were we ever surprised after the

Plague! In fact, up to that point there were wagers all across the near galaxy, the odds having been quite heavy in favor of Mankind annihilating himself altogether. High stakes changed hands over that one!"

"You mean, you actually use money?" you ask Adavan, shifting in your chair, as you look him initially in the eyes, then glance to your left.

"No, I just wanted to let you know we have a sense of humor!" he chuckles, his eyes tear and his fifth appendage vigorously moves in a circular arc; he also knocks the end of one of his upper extremities on the table, twice. "But there were bets and there were spoils to the winners. Not all jackpots are as valueless as a fiat currency or even other materials however pure or rare. But if you think those were huge, when Mankind did not abandon himself into oblivion, the stakes went up geometrically over what would happen next."

"Pardon me, Ambassador," you ask, "But are you a race of gamblers?"

"Ha, ha, that's a good one. I have to get up from your gracious chair and walk around for a moment and catch my breath." He breathes hard from his excitement, and his tongue hangs out slightly. "I can tell we will have much in common, personally and between our peoples," he continues, then returns to his seat. "We speculate as much as your Species does, an infrequent diversion that can provide periodic amusement, particularly where the statisticians are concerned. We have followed your bookmakers watching the hyperbolic drop off in the probability of finding other sentient Species in space who possess ISDs. Like with everything else in life, even though growth appears and is in fact continuous, the progress is indeed discontinuous and stepwise. One moment you can't do something or understand something; the next you can; same thing with ideas. But we can discuss temporal dynamics some other time.

"Yes, what would happen next? With the subsequent evolution of Mankind, we weren't surprised by your enlightened treatment of the inhabitants of other Worlds, clandestinely observing and learning from them without interaction unless you had come across a rare world that, despite not having ISDs, had achieved sufficient decorum so as to follow the two basic rules. Usually technology leads illumination, we have found."

Not knowing where this is going, you remain silent and attentive. The Ambassador continues, "This is the half Jubilee anniversary of your development of ISDs, right?"

"Yes, you obviously know it is," you calmly respond, your arms now folded in front of you, your fingers interlaced.

"The galactic community has been disappointed that all this time there has never been closure and the record set straight. In fact, no headway has been made at all in addressing a fundamental question about your people. We have never seen this before; thus we have given you so much time."

"What record? Question about what?" you ask. "You clearly know more about us than we do!" you say, extending your right arm in front of you, toward him, your hand straight, with fingers very slightly flexed, the tips just barely touching the table.

"Your transformation, of course. The origin of your Society after the great Plague." At this point, his fifth appendage is no longer moving, and has dropped downward toward the ground; his ears remain down, but curl slightly and move back; both forearms rest on the table. He reaches forward and gently touches your hand. His hair is so soft and silky, that you can't help running some strands through your finger tips, this curiously providing you with a great sense of well being. He doesn't appear to mind.

"We are fully aware of the implications of the Plague and how Mankind has changed for the better since then; this is taught in our schools to all Eartherians," you respond, hoping that you don't sound defensive.

"Understanding implications and subsequent changes are one thing, but you really don't fathom what happened with the Plague, do you?" Not waiting for an answer, he goes on. "Your DNA is some of the most robust we have ever encountered for a Species as young as yours. Why is that? Do you have the same chromosomes that you have always had?"

"No."

"And why is that?" He removes his hand from yours, to rub a spot on his shoulder.

"We don't know," you reply, your eyebrows raising. You also resume your posture with arms in front of you, but you glance at your shoulder and then at his which he is continuing to massage. "It was something we never investigated after the Plague. There were billions dead; much had to be done. Out of deference to the deceased, we felt it most opportune to leave well enough alone; we didn't want to waste time finding out what happened once it was clear that the infestation had burned itself out. We turned our resources elsewhere at that point."

"What do you call yourselves, your Species? And by what synonyms do you hail?"

"We are Homo sapiens, man the wise, also known as humanity or Mankind."

"That is correct, of course, but inaccurate, to be sure. Tell me what you know about Pawkey Seneschal."

"Who? I've never heard of him," you say, your eyes widening, then narrowing, as you think. "One moment, please. Computer," you call out, tossing your head back slightly and looking up.

"Yes, Minister," comes the vapid salutation unchanged for hundreds of Rotations, a comforting assurance of data to come.

"Please provide all information available concerning Pawkey Seneschal," you command.

"Yes, Minister Esse." There is a two billion picosecond pause. "There are no records concerning Pawkey Seneschal, by that name, for the last 7000 Rotations."

You roll your hands over on the table, shift in your seat again, grimace slightly and raise your eyebrows, looking again at Adavan.

"That's the problem," notes the Ambassador, his fifth

appendage picking up steam again. "You, Minister, all of your Race, need to know who Pawkey Seneschal was. The story all starts with him. Since we do not ask questions in these circumstances without knowing the answers in advance, we have prepared a re-creation of events at the time. Witness for yourselves the true origin of your Society. The Consortium demands your attention and Reconciliation at this time. We wish to have the record straight, so there is no more delusional subterfuge, albeit unintentional. We wish to welcome you to our Consortium, but insist that any member Races know their true roots. We do not worry that you will eventually deteriorate into barbarism again. No, we know that would never happen. But to not acknowledge the past is to remain naïve. Despite the outcome, the mechanism must be elucidated definitively, so that the costs of change, however large or small, are at least addressed. Your reverence, as reason for your lack of further Analysis, has been misplaced. If the piper is not paid, your race will become pariahs in the intergalactic community and shunned hereafter. Not only will you not see us, we will no longer provide any assistance as we have willingly done so often in the past. We trust you will do the right thing, given your nature, once you are presented with the facts concerning Dr. Seneschal. Consider now what you must. Minister Esse, if you will be serving refreshments, I would love some Water that is carbonated and sweet, but not fattening (of course)."

With that, all CDs, all formats regardless of size or device, begin broadcasting, including those where you are meeting with Ambassador Adavan. You order drinks and settle into your seat. The walls have changed color once.

# Book 9 Scientist III

YOUR LIFE HASN'T been the same since you woke up that morning with your idea. You understand the problem; you plan to do something about it, but first you need money. Big money; really big money.

Where else but the markets can you acquire phenomenal wealth over a relatively short period of time? Although the securities and futures industries have their share of crooks, this can be done quite legally. You do your homework and teach yourself the fundamentals; there are many ups and downs in your accounts. You finally identify the most important factor that must be achieved before success, as defined in these terms, is won. With faith and courage you follow your system, the fractal nature of all financial data, particularly those not subject to the whims of the printing press, dictating the patterns. Those who do not believe continue to hand their money to you. There are any number of games to be played; you find your favorites. You don't get greedy; you don't hope; you don't pray; you don't overtrade; you define your risk; you let profits run, but with a plan not to give back any more than you must. You follow the saw of buy low and sell high, using the financial data to define these terms, understanding that some things can go to zero or near zero, always going lower than you might ever imagine possible, or higher. These levels also define when to be contrary and when not. You define breakouts, expecting them to fail and then assess the implications when they do or do not. These can be further delineated by viewing the problem three dimensionally over different time frames. The one thing that you can rely on is the reproducible choices that must play out at certain crossroads; just about every game that you play goes up or down to a certain degree every year. That's all you have to know; world experts, with all the data at their disposal, haven't the faintest idea which way prices will really go; hence, how can you even pretend to know as much as they do or as much as the entities that actually produce or use the underlying assets or instruments?

Time is required; so is patience. Fortunes are lost quickly and made slowly. The money accumulates and grows.

Fifteen years later. You have sufficient funds.

This is an infrequent night for you now, one of not sleeping well; you wake up instantly recalling the nightmare about the bitch wife. She got her ass kicked out long ago, but it had to be what she had wanted. Why else would she have relentlessly tormented you for so long? She forced your hand, which you knew would be the defining moment when you ceased to be in love with her. There will always be a part of you that loves her, since you loved her so deeply at one time. You realize now that you grew apart; probably she was never the right person for you in the first place. The years of the second marriage were the worst of your entire life; though you told her this point blank, she still did not act. You have read that many people have a perversion to subconsciously want to fail; perhaps she was one of them.

Since her departure, you haven't been doing the masculine version of eating bon-bons and painting your toenails; rather you have been using portions of the moolah to begin implementing your plan. Fortuitously, but unnecessary in your overall design, certain markets plunge, it being that point in the financial destiny of all markets; your winnings magnify far over. This allows your time table to be advanced. You have already located the real estate, prepared architectural plans, received bids from contractors, and begun hiring personnel.

You buy the island far from any prying eyes. During these times of extreme global economic ruin, starvation, depravation, no one gives a shit what you do or where you do it as long as your money is the right karat and the denominations are large enough. It is amazing what money can buy; it is amazing what money can't buy, you find!

You install the buildings, move in the equipment; the workers arrive and business begins. The island is essentially self-sufficient, with recycling facilities and five year supplies of energy. There is plenty of money given the global depression; you manage to make even more, buying the premier companies, the survivors that are 90% off their peak prices. A couple go belly up, but the rest turn into "whatever is needed" to keep the island running, and then some.

There are twelve housing facilities, each holding 1200 people, all private rooms with shared bathroom facilities. There are additional private bathrooms in the common areas, where one can be relatively anonymous if the children gang up, pestering to go to the pool. Still, there is plenty of privacy as needed or desired, and all workers have whatever diversions they enjoy so long as they don't interfere with their occupations.

Monthly shipments of supplies and new workers come. Some jobs because of their nature, have marked turnover, about 10,000 per month. You have agents throughout the Globe recruiting, which is not hard during these destitute times. Everyone on the island has a job, all different of course, as much as each person is an individual. Many have the identical job description in order to allow an appropriate sample size for each of the experiments; the logistics have been painstakingly worked out. There are 10 million square feet of laboratory work space.

All the scientists you hire, each performs a tiny piece of work, a miniscule question in your overall design, though there are a very few who have been there from nearly the beginning: a few of the pleasantly obsequious, those without original ideas who earn their keep by doing the hard lifting without question, the truly faithful. Some will be Survivors, some won't.

The first major question you address is cellular aging

and death. You deconstruct the telomeric clock, one gear and spring at a time, until the blueprint of each piece is traced back to the genetic origins, assessing perturbations that allow for adjusting the speed of the mechanism, in either direction. After that, everything else is just a matter of time.

The expenditures are astronomical; it doesn't matter; the only goal is finding the truth. Experiment after experiment is designed, executed, analyzed, refined, tested again, and then repeated until a final conclusion is reached. This being biologic research, all animal models are treated in the most humane way possible, with suffering minimized if not expunged altogether. You have always followed this creed. The antivivisectionists won out decades ago, and the life sciences pretty much ground to a halt everywhere else.

Fifty years later. As part of your design, many children are conceived and born on the island. You address all the issues and questions, including, but not limited to, the very nature of thought, intelligence, imagination, morals, trust, fear, heroism, judgment, memory, ambition, hunger, passion, love, lust and erotica, compassion, music, abstraction, eye contact, faithfulness, gratitude, gluttony, greed, envy, rage, sloth, pride, despair, drug addiction, instinct, intuition, perception, sleep, dreams, nightmares, fine/repetitive movements, conception, pleasure, pain, smell and taste, reasoning, guilt, humor, joy, frustration, disappointment, charity, honor, commitment, xenophobia, contentment, lying, free-will, sentience, hypocrisy, consciousness.

By this time, the bay is full with the unrecyclable ashes, the burned calcium remains of the work product of the island. The island has a tiny dimpled area where once stood a deep harbor at the semicircular base of this edifice above the Water.

You are getting tired. You know you could go on much longer, but you decided, when you first awakened with your idea, that you would not take that opportunity. Your work is almost done anyways.

The final product is at hand. You knew it could be done with the right tools, equipment, and help. You are pleased with the solution; it is relatively elegant if you do say so yourself. But then, you've always liked your own cooking, too.

You have designed a tiny, extra chromosome. This controls the aging process, making cellular homeostasis more robust, with monitors of statistical events, like intracellular accumulations or deficiencies. Compensation is accomplished by replacing the bad portion of DNA, thus obliterating most disease; infections are fought in a more aggressive way, always adapting to new strains rather than the other way around. Regeneration is now marked. Also, each of the other chromosomes has a fractional portion of this 47th chromosome at one end. Should there be a problem with the 47th, they will break off and reform the missing, normal extra one which would then direct the others to synthesize more spare parts.

Your research is not cloning, however, and you will have nothing to do with it. The whole concept of duplicating a person is absurd, unless you could do it from the current person, by digitizing them in some science fiction type hocus pocus that would spit out an exact copy, as they stand today, with their current memories. Otherwise, you have a genetically identical person who will respond differently given the changed nature of the childhood environment in this world. This was concluded during your research, of course. What other conclusion could possibly be drawn, you had postulated, as you drew up the paradigms for investigating this further?

You inscribe a message in marble, imported from Rome, for placement inside a cave that is high above the bay near the top of the island facing leeward so as to be least disturbed by Wind and Water. Curiously, during all those years, no hurricane or other natural disaster has occurred. The message, which has been encoded, helped you get your shit together:

alfatdeheabhelewcahblealcandesmothysifbrycabularrca
rphebaribevilabyldmologbalcehenbeleefsybsaampodehacco

kuppeeirrabencameallegyogavelobatboedulphraccalaperari
fraufinthawetecjobchoupmadsirchabttoapiefaftyboishycha
ptdepluhcenieblamcyipeecdiclapcundedowmis Author not recalled. [DJS: Having solved this puzzle, I can assure you it is as accurate as it is amusing; but solving this or not, will not enhance nor detract, from one's overall appreciation and understanding of this translation.]

Soon you will unleash what will be remembered early on as Armageddon. The virus will be ferried about by Wind and Water; you will sleep after that and not awaken further. There will be no records or other tangible proof of your work. In the coming days, prior to activation of the virus, all property on the island, save the marble tablet, will self destruct, collapsing into piles of rubble that will effortlessly blow to the Four Corners.

When the virus strikes, it will affect everyone in the same sleep cycle, even alleged insomniacs since it will stay dormant long enough to catch all outliers. Thereafter, the DNA from the virus will incorporate itself into all cells of the body; the scumbags will be identified and destroyed.

In less than eight hours, over half of the human population of Earth will be gone. Their bodies will disintegrate, as tissue turns to dust, Water fleeing from all cells, returning to Wind, which will blow the remaining, disassembled atoms around the Globe. No one will be spared exposure. They will either transform, or they will vanish, as if they never existed in the first place.

There will be survivors who still die in the coming weeks or months, and they will be buried. These will be the few who had been irreversibly damaged prior to the Armageddon, to such a degree that even regeneration cannot overcome the brain destruction. Others who have been anywhere from ill but asymptomatic, to on death's door, will miraculously recover. They will continue to live in good health. The majority of survivors will have been fine prior to the virus; this won't be a case of only the infirm make it, to inherit Earth so to speak.

Those left will be evenly distributed over the sexes. Typically, they will be aggressive, motivated, curious, but with kindness in their hearts. The latter will perhaps be the one dominant characteristic of those who survive. These might in fact include the occasional criminal if there is true repentance; and other sinners, since virtually no one on Earth is truly without inappropriate crossness or lying, at some point in their lives past the age of early childhood. Naturally, any tobacco addicts who survive, and that will be a higher percentage than many previous cynics would have expected, won't light up or get a "chaw" upon awakening the next day. They will have no desire whatsoever.

Everyone will be able to understand everyone else, regardless of previous language. In fact, none of the previous languages will still exist. A contemporary language will be born, fully consisting of the best parts of each of the newly dead tongues, written into the language portions of the brain. You have no idea what they will call this, but their children will still pick this up, verbally, during infancy. A simple working version of this written language will need to be codified in the days after the virus has burned out, after it is clear what has happened and what needs to be done to keep things rolling. Like all languages, this will remain a work in progress. Innuendo and ambiguity will also survive, but language impediments will no longer be a source of friction in the family of Mankind.

Of those who are blown into oblivion, the loss will indeed be global, but nowhere will there be a higher per capita loss than the southeastern portion of the northern continent in the western hemisphere. To be sure there will be annihilation of entire genealogies wherever there are human sewers, regardless of affluence; the primary targets being obviously the scumbags, at least by your definition. This sanitization of Mankind will flush the incorrigibles, the truly wicked once and for all.

There will be no more thimblerigging, purblind bureaucrats or lawyers; no cynics or pessimists; those addicted to government, who are selfish, who hate, who bully and taunt, none of these will make it past that last bit of sleep they have. They will experience horrible nightmares prior to their demise.

Given the nature and transformation of the survivors, there will be no murder, rape, molestation, beating, assault, or any other violent or white collar crime. Everyone will be reasonably reasonable, there now being only two basic rules; these will cover every situation. Even stupidity, a precursor for arrogance, will be removed, no longer blemishing the face of Earth, the exquisite nature of which will be acknowledged by all.

The remaining, well, they will have their whole lives ahead of them, as their bodies and minds grow and evolve in conjunction with their DNA transformations, lives long enough to get done just about anything they choose, just as yours has been.

# Book 10 Minister III

YOU ARE AWESTRUCK, as is your entire Race. You control yourself from making a gaping "O" with your mouth. There is a complete hush over the Planet. The implications are astounding. How would you have ever known? You sniff and blink your eyes a few times, waiting for Adavan to speak. You adjust your chair. The tiles have changed colors twice. You move your arms in front of you again, resting on the table, with fingers loosely interlaced.

"Impressive, huh?" asks the Ambassador, his head bobbing again. He also shifts in the seat before getting up again to walk around the perimeter of the room, three times. His arms move in multiple directions, each unrelated to the other, without apparent purpose other than muscle stimulation; his fifth appendage has also curled up and is moving horizontally, rather rapidly. He then sits down and finishes his refreshments, having asked for seconds at the intermission. "So that's 3 billion scumbags dead; 5 billion, at this point, wonderful enlightened souls; north of 7 million lives, the cost of transformation. In your ancient religious literature, an aphorism equates the saving of an individual with the salvation of your entire Race. If this is so, the implications of the converse are indeed frightening.

"The Facts: Dr. Seneschal recruited desperate employees who didn't know what they were getting themselves into, be they on the giving or getting end of the experiments. Although sexual reproduction continued to be required for some issues, early employees aided development of completely in vitro conception and fetal development. The millions of people available thereafter allowed for the most intimate questions, the testing matrices being custom designed from inception, literally. Despite the gargantuan number differential, we of the Consortium believe you have been mourning, so to speak, with your reverence for the Plague, the wrong people. Seven million people cashed in their lives for your extra chromosome. What say you now?"

You look him in the eyes, yours reflecting the epiphany as well as deep sorrow that is in your heart; but your determination is not lost on him either. "Obviously, and I am sure I speak for all my people, it is clear that we must move forward and acknowledge our origins. Anytime there is loss of life, especially sentient, we are mournful..."

"And rightfully so," blurts the Ambassador interrupting you; his head and fifth appendage are moving in synchrony, something you haven't seen thus far. "This is one of your many enduring virtues. Your Species enjoys and actually builds relationships with 'dumb animals.' There are some in the Consortium who think that is so cute. Anyway, where were we? Yes, go on. I apologize; the bubbles make us a little giddy."

"I believe we can make a Reconciliation that will satisfy your Consortium. I have been thinking about this during your re-creation of the events of the Plague and Dr. Seneschal. I propose that all previous holidays commemorating War and heroes of those horrible interchanges of Mankind be abolished. I propose that yesterday and today be marked as new days of celebration, marking our introduction to the Consortium. And finally, I propose that the story of Pawkey Seneschal be written and told to our people henceforth, a few paragraphs of our exodus from xenophobia to be read aloud everyday and taught to all our children as part of their earliest memories."

"Those are outstanding resolutions," Adavan says after a soft belch. Wiping his mouth, this being a slightly liquid eructation, the Ambassador goes on, "There is still the problem of your chromosomes, don't you think? But I am sure the details of that can be worked out. Your Species is past the half-way point toward transcending this dilemma and restoring tranquility to your world."

* * * * * * * * * * *

"WHAT DID HE mean?" asked Wind. He and Water had been observing this interchange since the beginning. They were excited for their offspring with this great opportunity at hand. They had maintained a very low profile during the re-creation.

"You know," said Water. "Or, at least you should if you had been paying attention." She was cavorting in a fountain, outside the Council Center. It was circular and about a hundred streams from the periphery were aimed at the center. With Wind and Sun both massaging her droplets, she was feeling particularly effervescent.

"I was. I've just got a lot on my mind these days," he wambled.

"Sure you do! But your discomfiture is at the other end after the drubbing you've been through. You're just now realizing my stealth boot up your ass!"

"But you cheated!" exhorted Wind. "Mankind is no longer around."

"But he is," Water rejoined, not trying to be thrasonical. "I grant you humanity is now hufemity and the Species can no longer taxonomically be named Homo sapiens, man the wise. Rather, now mankind, if you will, has evolved into Femina persapiens, woman the wiser. QED."

"I still feel you cheated," sputtered Wind. But then as was his nature, he went on, "Let's go to the Equator and fool around."

"Oh goody! But I did not."

"Did too."

"Did not."

"Did too...."

"Did not...."

# Lexicon

akathisia—an inability to sit still, being constantly in movement

as if—an expression of low probability that approaches "forget about it," as well as NFW**

borborygmi—intestinal sounds made by moving gases and other contents

buttfucker—one who calls the dogs over after he has picked his nose; it's one thing to flick it away and let chance and the nature of the dog take their course

CD, perfect—one that allows you to look up or watch or attend to anything that you would like to look up or watch or attend to whenever you would like to look up, watch or attend to it, with bookmarks and file saving capacity

Church, the—as opposed to the Synagogue, Mosque, Temple

cooter—abdominal fat

DCD—domiciliary communication device

dollar—see skunk

donkey—ass

drinks, soft—see soda

Fire—the outlier that doesn't require genderfication

FLFs—funny looking fucks

fuck, fucking, fucked—nothing original here, previously acknowledged to be the all purpose word of all time, imitated by some for politeness with another word beginning with "f" or with just the letter "f" by itself, but one knows better; often incredulous dismay; sexual intercourse; to experience a less than desired outcome

GDMFSOB—goddamn mother fucking son of a bitch

HNIC—head nigger in charge

igged—ignored

ISDs—interstellar drives

lattice—electronic network that provides seamless, wired and wireless communications and entertainment, from one location to another or virtually limitless others marriage, bad—one in which you still have sex because it feels good, but you'd just as soon be doing it with a fuck buddy who at least responds with enthusiasm befitting someone who cares for you

mofo—need one ask

neoplasia—tumors, either malignant or benign

NFW—no fucking way

niggers—scumbags who are black

outlier—one who is out of touch from the mainstream, perhaps to the point of being weak and thus vulnerable to derision

PCD—personal communication device

potch—a very gentle spank

PWTs—scumbags who are white

rat, dying like a—while fucking

religion—too often it comes down to little more than this: Humor section of Temple newspaper: Joey was at the back of the synagogue last night, cutting up with the other youngsters his age. Rabbi was talking about the latest, greatest, Hollywood religious extravaganza, a sure hit in the cycle of redundancy, given the vast audience on which to draw; you can imagine the merchandising to be had. The fact that Jewish businesses are shut out of the bidding for said paraphernalia is not the reason for Rabbi's fluster; no, he is more afraid of an anti-Semitic backlash and said he would under no circumstances pay any amount of money to see his ancestors be blamed, once again. Little Joey, half listening, was heard to have said, "Hey guys, I'd gladly spend five bucks; how often do you get the opportunity to see the shit being beaten out of Jesus?" And the Muslims say, "Look, we know they hate our guts too, but at least they don't blame the death of that SonofaBitch on us." And those on the other side of the World, who have an entirely different spirituality, they say, "Leave us out entirely; we think you're all nuts, although at least some of you make sense and are relatively benign."

Rotations—solar cycles

scumbags—any worthless human being
shit—stuff, could be good or could be bad; exclamation of epiphany or rapture, or just the opposite (which then usually means you're fucked); excrement
SHPOS—subhuman piece of shit
skunk, see dollar
soda—Water that is carbonated and sweet, but not fattening (of course)
SSDD—same shit, different day
tard—if you don't know this one, you're "it" and shouldn't be reading this book
trinities, unholy—typically in the singular; a classic metaphor depicting the sad similarity between any three entities or situations that have an additional commonality of being "bad"
womanhood, five level hierarchy of— (in descending order), wife, fiancée, lover, whore, slut
YYW—yeah, yeah, whatever

# Translator's Commitment

D.J. SOLOMON, AS the translator of this version of Xen, commits to give ten percent (10%) of all proceeds generated by this work, in any capacity, after expenses, and before taxes, for his lifetime, to four (4) charities, the gifts to be made annually, the first bequests marking the one year anniversary of the publication, December 2006, upon timely audit. Confirmation of this will be available from the accounting firm, upon SASE request to the publisher. Charities sharing some of Xen's tenets may apply for funding by contacting the publisher, for further information.

# The Puzzle

HINTS:

1. The puzzle is based on a simple, repeating algorithm.
2. A computing device is not required, but an instrument for making notes is.
3. As in the puzzle itself, the letters of the final solution are one continuous set, without spaces between words, but the message can easily be read by all who have a knowledge of common Ancient English.
4. While probably multiple messages can be found by manipulation of the code, there is only one “correct” answer in keeping with the original Xen, in Eartherian.

LaVergne, TN USA
21 September 2009

158559LV00002B/151/A